PINOCCHIO

THE ADVENTURES OF A LITTLE WOODEN BOY

by *Carlo Collodi*

ILLUSTRATED BY RICHARD FLOETHE

INTRODUCTION BY MAY LAMBERTON BECKER

TRANSLATED BY JOSEPH WALKER

Philomel Books
New York

First paperback edition published 1982 by
Philomel Books
a division of The Putnam Publishing Group
200 Madison Avenue, New York, N.Y. 10016
Library of Congress Cataloging in Publication Data
Collodi, Carlo, 1826–1890.
Pinocchio, the adventures of a little wooden boy.
Translation of: Le avventure di Pinocchio.
Reprint. Originally published: Cleveland: World
Pub. Co. 1946. (Rainbow classics)
Summary: The adventures of a talking wooden
marionette whose nose grew whenever he told a lie.
[1. Fairy tales.   2. Puppets and puppet-plays—
Fiction]   I. Floethe, Richard, ill.   II. McSpadden,
J. Walker (Joseph Walker), 1874–1960.   III. Title.
PZ8.L887Pi 1982   [Fic]   82-549
ISBN 0-399-20892-5 (pbk.)   AACR2
Printed in the United States of America.

RAINBOW CLASSICS

General Editor: May Lamberton Becker

Contents

CONTENTS

How this book came to be written

by May Lamberton Becker

HIS name was really Carlo Lorenzini, but when he wrote *Pinocchio* it was under the name of Collodi, which is a little village in Tuscany. He himself lived in Florence; by his own account he must have been as mischievous as his hero when he went to school. The pupils in his class were seated in two sections; on the right were the "Romans," and on the left the "Carthaginians." At regular intervals the boy who stood at the head of his group would be crowned "Emperor" of his side. Even Collodi was Emperor once, but he says it was "a passing glory," for in two hours' time the crown was lifted from his head and a dunce cap took its place. You see, he was the sort of pupil who kept the others asking, "Teacher, will you make Collodi stop?"

Now there was a friend of his named Sylvan,

fat as a turkey, who came one day to school in a pair of new white trousers. Sylvan loved to sleep, even more in school than at home, and when that morning he leaned over as usual and dozed off, the chance to draw a beautiful picture was too much for his seatmate to resist.

"So without losing any time, I began to draw on his trousers as far as I could reach. I drew a lovely soldier on a horse. The horse's mouth was wide open, just about to eat a big fish, so that you could understand it was Friday. To tell you the truth, I liked it more each time I looked at my sketch.

"Alas, it didn't impress my friend Sylvan that way."*

These tricks went on till the teacher put him out of both Empires and made him sit at a desk alone. For a while he kept on, even there, being the bright bad boy of the class—until he began to wonder if it were really so bright to think up tricks that only got him and everyone else into trouble. The teacher was no longer begged to make Collodi stop, for he stopped all by himself —and somewhat to his own surprise, was made an Emperor again.

He grew up, held government positions, was decorated for valor in war, and started a little

* Quoted in *The Junior Book of Authors* (H. W. Wilson Co.)

newspaper. How he came to write for children we learn from his countryman, Giuseppe Prezzolini, who wrote for the *Saturday Review of Literature* one of the very few articles about Collodi that have appeared in English. We find that Lorenzini wrote dramatic criticisms and sketches, and was over fifty when Felix Poggi asked him to translate three of Perrault's fairy tales from the French. These were so popular that he was then asked to try something of his own for children, and produced a new kind of school book that for a little while made study amusing to children.

In 1881, the *Children's Journal* was started at Rome, and a friend of our author became its secretary. One day this man received a batch of papers with a note from Collodi telling him to do what he liked with "this bit of foolishness." It happened to be the first adventure of Pinocchio. Children immediately demanded another ... and another ... and Collodi wrote them just as they came into his head, and sent them in as it struck his fancy to do so. In book form, a million copies were sold in Italy alone. Other countries received them with open arms. It was translated into all languages, including the Gaelic and Japanese.

Yet you might have thought the little puppet so thoroughly Italian that children in other lands would not understand his charm. For if you have ever seen a performance at an Italian puppet theatre, you would know that the audience feels that the puppets in it are as alive as those who watch and applaud them. Each province in Italy has created a marionette that gives other people an idea of its own characteristics, such as Pantalone of Venice, Stenterello of Florence, or Gianduia of Turin. There is a story called *Puppet Parade*, written by Carol Della Chiesa (who also made a translation of *Pinocchio*), in which all the puppets of Italy gather in Florence to choose a king. Some are centuries old; and they look down upon a newcomer with skinny legs, a pert look and a long nose. But when the parade starts, and the crowd of children vote by throwing wreaths at the puppet they love best, Pinocchio gets so many that he has to hang them on his long nose. Everyone cries out that he is not only King of the Puppets of Italy, but the Pinocchio of the whole world.

I'm sure they were right. Benedetto Croce, a famous philosopher, has said: "The wood out of which Pinocchio is carved is humanity itself."

Which means, I think, that all of us human beings also make mistakes, atone for them, get into and out of trouble, and keep on trying to make our dreams come true. I don't wonder children love Pinocchio. He's so much like them.

Richard Floethe, the artist who made the pictures for this edition, must have been a good deal like Collodi when he was a boy (and like Pinocchio, too). His first attempts as an artist were at drawing caricatures of his teachers in his school books. He studied art in Dortmund, then at the Academy at Munich, and the Bauhaus at Weimar, learning the techniques of woodcut, lithograph, book design and typography. One of his teachers foretold that he would one day become an illustrator. His first commission after leaving art school was to paint a large mural at the International Exposition at Cologne in 1928. This was no sooner finished than he sailed for the United States. He has lived here ever since, and has become an American citizen.

Floethe has illustrated many, many stories for children and for their elders, too, and you have seen his work on book jackets and in advertising displays. He is well known as a water colorist.

and some of his works in this medium, as well as his prints, are to be found in large art galleries and museums. Twice he has won the Limited Editions Club Contest for the best illustrated book.

PINOCCHIO

1 A Stick of Wood
That Talked

ONCE upon a time there was—

"A king!" my little readers will say at once.

No, my dears, you are wrong. Once upon a
time there was a stick of wood. It was not a fine

15

stick, either, but just such another as you would put in the fireplace to heat the room.

I do not know how it came about, but one fine day this stick of wood was found in the carpenter shop of an old man named Antonio. Everybody called him Master Cherry, however, because of the color of his nose which was red and shiny like a ripe cherry.

As soon as Master Cherry saw the stick of wood he was delighted. He rubbed his hands together and mumbled to himself: "The very thing! This stick will make a fine table leg."

Saying this, he picked up a sharp axe to begin to smooth off the bark; but just as he was about to strike he stopped with arm in air, for he thought he heard a thin sharp voice cry out: "Do not strike me too hard!"

Imagine good old Master Cherry's surprise! He rolled his eyes around in every corner of the room to see whence came the voice, but could discover no one. He looked under the workbench; nobody. He looked into the tightly-shut cupboard; nobody. He looked into the chip basket and shavings; nobody. He opened the door and looked up and down the street; but still nobody. What then?

"Ah, I see!" he laughed to himself and scratched his wig. "I only dreamed that I heard a voice. Let's begin again."

He took up the axe again and hit the stick of wood a lively blow.

"Ouch! You have hurt me!" cried the little voice in pain.

This time Master Cherry stood as if turned to stone, his eyes fairly sticking out of his head, his tongue hanging out of his mouth for all the world like a gorgon head on a fountain. As soon as he found his voice he said, trembling and stammering:

"Who was it that cried out? There is not a living soul here. Is it possible that this stick can cry like a baby? I can't believe it. It's just like any other piece of wood that you put on the fire to boil a pot of beans. What then? Can somebody be hidden inside? If so, so much the worse for him. I'll fix him!"

So saying he laid hold of the poor stick of wood and began to pound it against the wall. Then he paused to listen if any one should cry out. He listened for two minutes—nothing; for five minutes—nothing; for ten minutes, and still nothing.

"Ah, I see!" he tried to laugh again and scratch his wig; "this little voice that called 'Ouch!' was only my imagination. Let's begin again."

And because he had really begun to be frightened, he tried to hum a tune to keep up his courage. At the same time he laid his axe aside and took up a plane, in order to smooth and polish the wood; but he had no sooner begun to push it back and forth, when he heard the same sharp little voice say with a laugh: "Stop you are tickling me!"

This time, poor Master Cherry fell down as if thunderstricken. When he opened his eyes he found himself seated upon the ground. His face was blank with amazement, and the end of his nose had changed from red to blue because of his great alarm.

2 Master Cherry Gives the Stick to Gepetto

AT this moment a knock was heard on the door.

"Come in," said the carpenter, who did not have strength enough to get up.

A little old man whose name was Gepetto entered. He was often called Polendina by the bad boys who wished to tease him, on account of his yellow wig which looked like a bag of yellow meal. You must know, that is what "polendina" means in Italy, and it always made him angry to be called this.

"Good morning, Antonio," said Gepetto, "what are you doing on the ground?"

"I am teaching the ants to read."

"May it do you good!"

"What has brought you here, friend Gepetto?" asked the other in his turn.

"My legs. But I would like to ask a favor of you."

"At your service," replied the carpenter, beginning to rise.

"This morning an idea popped into my head."

"Let's have it."

"I thought to myself that I would carve out a clever marionette of wood; and with this marionette, which I can teach to dance and do tricks, I can wander about over the world and earn my living. What do you think?"

"Bravo, Polendina!" cried a sharp little voice.

On hearing this nickname, Gepetto grew as

red as a pepper, and turned upon the carpenter saying harshly, "What do you mean by insulting me?"

"I never insulted you!"

"You called me Polendina."

"Indeed I did not."

"Don't you think I can believe my ears? I heard you."

"No!"

"Yes!"

"No!"

"Yes!"

From words they soon came to blows, and scuffled about until each had seized the other by the wig.

"Give me back my wig!" cried Antonio.

"Then give me mine, and let us make peace," said Gepetto.

So the two foolish old fellows exchanged wigs, shook hands again, and promised to be good friends for the rest of their lives.

"And now, friend Gepetto," said the carpenter, "what is the favor you desire of me?"

"I need a piece of wood, from which to carve my marionette. Can you give me one?"

Master Antonio was glad enough to go after

the stick of wood which had already given him so much alarm. But when he tried to hand it over to his friend, the wood gave a kick and sliding out of his hands landed violently upon the shins of poor Gepetto.

"Ah, you are not very polite when you give presents, Master Antonio," he groaned. "You have nearly lamed me."

"Upon my word, I didn't do it!"

"Then I suppose *I* must have!"

"The fault is all in that wood."

"Oh, I know the wood hit me—but you threw it at my legs."

"No, I did not throw it."

"Scoundrel!"

"Gepetto, don't insult me, or I shall call you Polendina."

"Donkey!"

"Polendina!"

"Monkey!"

"Polendina!"

"Ugly ape!"

"Polendina!"

Gepetto now thoroughly angry threw himself upon the carpenter and they fought it out to a finish. Antonio got his nose scratched, and Gepetto lost two buttons off his coat. Having thus squared accounts they shook hands solemnly and promised again to be good friends for the rest of their lives. Then Gepetto picked up the stick of wood, thanked Antonio, and limped back home.

3 How Pinocchio Was Made

GEPETTO's home was one small room on a ground floor under a staircase. Its furniture could not have been simpler: there was a tumble-down chair, a poor bed, and a ricketty table. There seemed to be a fireplace at the back, but it was only a picture, and so was the fire and the pot above it, which appeared to give out clouds of steam.

As soon as he reached home, Gepetto took up his tools and fell to work carving out his marionette.

"What name shall I give him?" he asked himself. "I think it shall be Pinocchio; that's a name which will bring him good luck. I once knew a whole family called Pinocchio, and all did well. The richest of the lot knew how to beg."

Now that he had found a name for his marionette, Gepetto fell hard to work and soon had carved the hair, then the top of the head, and then the eyes. No sooner had he made the eyes than—much to his surprise—the marionette moved them and began to stare at him!

Gepetto did not like this and said sharply:

"Why do you stare at me, wooden eyes?"

No reply.

Next he made the nose, but no sooner was it made than it began to grow. It grew and grew and grew as though it never would stop. Poor Gepetto tried to cut it short, but the more he chipped the longer that impudent nose became. So he let it alone and began on the mouth. But the mouth was not half done before it began to laugh and mock him.

"Stop your laughing!" scolded Gepetto; but it was like talking to the wall.

"Stop your laughing, I tell you!" he called loudly.

The mouth ceased its grinning, but began to make faces at him. Gepetto pretended not to see this, and went on with his work. After the mouth he made the chin, then the neck, the shoulders, the body, the arms and the hands.

No sooner had he made the hands than they grabbed the wig off of Gepetto's head. He turned quickly.

"Pinocchio!" he called, "put back my wig at once."

But instead of doing so, Pinocchio put it upon his own head, making himself look half smothered.

At this piece of insolence, Gepetto grew sad and thoughtful—something he had never been before in his life.

"You naughty little scamp!" he said; "you

are not all made yet, and already you begin to
lack respect for your father.   Bad, bad boy!"

And he wiped away a tear.

There were still legs and feet to be carved. The
moment Gepetto finished making them, he felt a
kick on the end of his nose.

"It's all my fault," he said to himself.   "I
ought to have thought of this at first.   Now it is
too late."

He took the marionette by the arms and stood
him up on the floor, in order to teach him to walk.
But Pinocchio's joints were stiff so that he could
hardly move them, and Gepetto had to lead him
about by the hand.   Pretty soon his legs grew
more limber, and Pinocchio began to run by himself around the room.   Finally, as the door was
open, he jumped through it and started at full
speed down the street.

Poor Gepetto went after him as hard as he
could but could not catch him, because the little
rascal ran by leaps and bounds like a rabbit, striking his wooden feet on the pavement with a lively
clatter.

"Stop him! stop him!" yelled Gepetto; but
the passers-by, seeing a wooden marionette

charging down the street like a Barbary horse, only stared and then laughed and laughed in a way you could hardly imagine.

At last by good luck a policeman came along who, hearing all the racket, thought that some colt was running away from his owner; and planting himself bravely in the middle of the street he decided to stop the runaway at all hazards. When Pinocchio saw him in the way he tried to get past by dodging between the officer's legs, but failed. The policeman without budging caught him by the nose—which was long enough for a handle—and turned him over to the panting Gepetto. The latter wanted to punish him by boxing his ears; but fancy his disappointment, when, after searching vainly he could find no ears to box! He had forgotten to make any!

So he contented himself with seizing the marionette by the nape of the neck, and led him back saying with an ominous shake of the head, "Just wait till I get you home! I'll give you a good one —never doubt it!"

When Pinocchio heard this he threw himself flat on the ground and would not stir another step. At once a group of idlers and curious people gathered around them—one saying one thing, another saying another.

"Poor Marionette!" quoth one, "he is right in not wanting to go home. Who knows how hard that Gepetto might beat him!"

Another added: "This Gepetto seems to be a good sort, but he is harsh with boys. If he gets this poor marionette into his hands, he might smash it to pieces."

Indeed, they all said so much that the policeman finally gave Pinocchio his liberty, and marched the unlucky Gepetto to jail. All the way there he wept and cried so that he wasn't able to plead his innocence. He could only wail: "Wicked son! To think that I took so much pains to make a *good* marionette! But it serves me right! I ought to have thought of this at first!"

What happened afterward is a very strange story. I know you could never guess, so I shall have to tell you in the chapters that come next.

4 The Talking Cricket

AND now, children, let me tell you how, while poor Gepetto was being taken to jail through no fault of his own, that rogue of a Pinocchio, freed by the policeman, ran across country in order to get home quickly. In his great haste he leaped over high walls and jumped ditches full of water exactly like a rabbit that is chased by the hunters.

When he reached home he found the street door open. He entered, fastened the door behind him, and then sat down on the ground with a sigh of relief. But his contentment did not last long, for presently he heard a voice in the room saying: "Creek, creek, creek!"

"Who's that?" demanded Pinocchio.

"It is I."

Pinocchio turned around and saw a large cricket crawling upon the wall.

"Tell me, Cricket, who are you?"

"I am the Talking Cricket, and I have lived in this room over a hundred years."

"But the room belongs to me now," said the Marionette, "and if you want to do me a favor you will go at once, without looking back."

"I will not go away until I've told you a great truth," answered the Cricket.

"Tell it then and be quick about it."

"It will go hard with boys who do not mind their parents and who run away from home.

They will never have any good luck, and sooner or later they will be sorry."

"Sing on, Cricket, if you want to. But I'm going to leave here the first thing in the morning, because I know, if I stay, the same thing will happen to me that happens to other boys. I shall have to go to school, and be made to study. And, between us, I don't care to study. I intend to play and to amuse myself by climbing trees and robbing birds' nests."

"Poor little stupid! Don't you know that by doing thus you will make a donkey of yourself, and that everybody will laugh at you?"

"Be still, croaking Cricket!" cried Pinocchio.

But the Cricket, who was wise and did not like such rudeness, continued in the same tone of voice: "If you dislike the idea of going to school, why not learn some trade so that you could earn an honest bit of bread?"

"Shall I tell you why?" replied Pinocchio impatiently. "Then know that there is only one trade in the world that would really suit me."

"And what trade is that?"

"That of eating, drinking, sleeping, playing, and leading an easy life all day long."

"That way of doing," said the Talking Cricket calmly, "always leads to a bad end."

"Be careful, croaking Cricket! If you make me angry, look out for yourself!"

"Poor Pinocchio! I pity you!"

"Why do you pity me?"

"Because you are only a marionette, and what is worse, you are a blockhead."

At this last word Pinocchio sprang up in a rage and seizing a heavy wooden mallet from the work-bench he threw it at the Talking Cricket. Perhaps he didn't really intend to hit it, but by ill luck it struck the Cricket back of the head, so that it had only time to cry, "Creek, creek, creek!" Then it was left sticking to the wall.

5 Pinocchio Suffers from Hunger

In the meantime night came on, and Pinocchio remembering that he had eaten nothing began to feel a gnawing in his stomach that was a good deal like an appetite. Now, appetites with boys grow very quickly, and in a few minutes it became a real hunger, and the hunger grew till it was like that of a wolf.

Pinocchio ran over to the hearth where the bean pot was boiling away, and tried to take off the lid to see what was inside. But the pot was only painted on the wall. Imagine his surprise! His long nose grew at least four inches longer.

Then he began to run around the room, searching through all the drawers and boxes for so much as a crust of bread, a bone for a dog, a cherry stone—anything to eat; but couldn't find the least thing. And all the time his hunger grew and kept on growing. Poor Pinocchio could do nothing but yawn, he was that empty, and his mouth stretched so that it reached to where his ears ought to be. He had a terribly vacant feeling. He began to weep and to wail, and said:

"The Talking Cricket was right. I was naughty to disobey my father and run away. If my father were only here now, I should not be dying from hunger. Oh, how bad I feel!"

At this moment behold! He saw over in the shavings something that looked round and white, like a hen's egg. At once he jumped for it and seized it. It was really an egg. The joy of the marionette is beyond description. Almost fearing it was a dream, he turned the egg over and over in his hands, petting and kissing it.

"How shall I cook it?" he said. "Shall I make an omelet, or shall I fry it in a pan? Perhaps I'd better boil it. No, the quickest way will be to cook it in the pan! I am in such a hurry to eat it."

At once he set about it. He started a little fire and put the pan over it. Instead of butter or oil, he used a little water; and when the water began to smoke, crack! He broke the shell and held the egg over the pan. But instead of the egg's white and yolk, out jumped a little chicken, gay and lively, who made him a bow and said:

"A thousand thanks, Mr. Pinocchio, for having saved me the trouble of breaking my shell. Pray give my regards to your family." And saying this it spread its wings and flew through the window and out of sight.

The marionette stood motionless with staring eyes, open mouth, and the broken egg-shell still in his hands. Then when he began to recover, he set up a loud howling and beat upon the ground.

"Oh, Talking Cricket, you were right!" he cried. "If only I hadn't run away! If only my

father were here!   I shall starve to death, I know
I shall!"

And as his stomach kept on hurting and he
didn't know what else to do, he decided to go out
and run to the village not far away, in the hope of
finding some kind-hearted person who would
give him a bit of bread.

6 Pinocchio Burns
His Feet Off

IT happened to be a stormy night. The thunder crashed, the lightning was so constant that the whole sky seemed ablaze, and a strong wind swept along a cloud of dust and shook every tree in the countryside.

Pinocchio was dreadfully afraid of the thunder and lightning; but his hunger was stronger than his fear. He opened the door, darted out, and in a hundred leaps reached the village out of breath and with his tongue hanging out of his mouth like a hunter's dog. But he found everything silent and deserted. The shops were closed, the house-doors closed, the windows closed, and there wasn't even a dog in the streets. It seemed like a city of the dead.

In despair Pinocchio rang the bell of the first house he came to, saying to himself: "Some one will surely answer."

Pretty soon an old man with a nightcap on his head looked out of a window and called gruffly: "What do you want at this hour of the night?"

"Would you be good enough to give me something to eat?"

"Wait a moment and I will be back!" replied the old man who thought that he was dealing with one of the street urchins who amuse themselves by ringing door-bells at night to rouse people out of their beds. In about half a minute he returned and said to Pinocchio: "Come under the window and hold up your hat."

Pinocchio had not yet owned a hat, but he drew close to the house, when a torrent of water from a large pitcher drenched him from head to foot. There was nothing to do but go back home, wet as a chicken, and tired and hungry. He threw himself down on a chair and rested his wet feet on the stove full of live coals.

There he fell asleep; and while he snored away, his feet being of wood soon became charred, then began to smoke, and finally burned clear off. But Pinocchio only slept and snored as though his feet belonged to somebody else.

Along toward morning he was awakened by a knocking at the door.

"Who is it?" he asked, yawning and rubbing his eyes.

"It is I," replied a voice.

It was the voice of Gepetto.

7 Gepetto Gives Pinocchio His Own Breakfast

POOR Pinocchio was so sleepy that he still did not know his feet were burned off. When he heard his father's voice he slid down from the chair to run and unbolt the door.   But instead he tottered for two or three steps and then fell flat on the floor.

"Let me in!" called Gepetto from the street.

"I can't, father," replied the marionette, weeping and rolling on the floor.

"Why not?"

"My feet have been eaten off."

"Who has eaten them?"

"The cat," said Pinocchio, seeing pussy in the corner playing with some pieces of wood.

"Let me in, I tell you," replied Gepetto; "else I shall give you a cat-o'-nine-tails instead."

"Believe me, I can't walk a step.   Oh, poor me, poor me!   I shall have to go round on my knees the rest of my life."

But Gepetto only thought this some trick of the marionette's; so to end the talk he climbed up the wall and entered the room through the window.   As first he scolded him severely; but when he saw Pinocchio lying on the floor without any feet, he was touched with pity.   He raised him up gently and began to pet him, saying tenderly:

"My dear little Pinocchio!   How did you happen to burn your feet off?"

"I don't know, father, but believe me, it has been a terrible night and one I shall never forget. It thundered and lightened and I was awfully hungry. Then along came a Talking Cricket who said, 'Serves you right!' and I said, 'Take care, Cricket!' and he said, 'You're a blockhead!' and I up with a mallet and smashed him on the wall. Then I tried to cook an egg, but instead a chicken flew out of it, thanking me kindly. And then I grew so hungry that I went over to the village and rang a bell, and a little old man said, 'Come under the window and hold up your hat,' and then he poured water all over me. I came back home in a hurry and stuck my feet on the stove to dry them, and while I was asleep they burned up. And now I haven't got any feet, and I'm *so* hungry! Oh, oh, oh, oh!"

And Pinocchio cried so loud you could have heard him for a mile.

His story was much mixed, but Gepetto caught the main point in it, which was the fact that the marionette was hungry. So he took three pears out of his pocket, saying, "Here are some pears which were to have been my own breakfast, but I will gladly give them to you. Eat them and may they do you good."

"If you want me to eat them, please peel them for me."

"Peel them?" replied Gepetto in surprise. "I would never have thought, my boy, that you would be so hard to please. One has to get used to all sorts of things in this world."

"You may be right," replied Pinocchio; "but I don't intend to eat any fruit that isn't peeled. I don't like the skins."

At this the good Gepetto took out a small knife and patiently peeled the three pears, laying all the peeling on a corner of the table.

When Pinocchio had eaten the first pear, he was on the point of throwing away the core, but Gepetto stopped him.

"Don't throw that away," he said; "everything is of some use."

"But I don't propose to eat cores."

"Very well," replied his father calmly.

But the cores, instead of being thrown away, were placed on the corner of the table with the parings.

Having eaten, or rather gobbled, the three pears, Pinocchio yawned and said with a whine, "Oh, dear, I am still hungry!"

"I haven't anything else, my boy."

"Really, truly nothing?"

"Nothing except these peelings and cores."

"All right then," said Pinocchio; "I guess I'd better eat some peeling."

He began to eat—at first with a wry face—but one after another the skins went down. Then he tackled the cores, and when he had finished the lot he said, patting his stomach contentedly, "Ah, I feel better!"

"You see, then," observed Gepetto, "that I was right when I told you everything was of some use in this world."

8 Gepetto Makes Another Pair of Feet for Pinocchio

As soon as the marionette's hunger was satisfied, he began to complain because he wanted a new pair of feet. Gepetto let him cry for a good while, in order to punish him; then he said:

"Why should I make you new feet?—So that you may run away from home again?"

"Oh, no! I promise to be good after this!" said Pinocchio sobbing.

"That's what all boys say when they want anything."

"I promise to go to school and to study so that you will be proud of me."

"That's what all boys say when they want anything."

"But I'm not like other boys. I am better than any of them. I always tell the truth. And I promise you, father, that I will learn a trade and be of some help to you."

Gepetto felt so sorry for him that he couldn't say another word. He took up some choice bits of wood and set to work so earnestly that in less than an hour he had carved out two beautiful new feet. They were so fine and graceful that they looked as though modeled by some great sculptor. Then he said to the boy, "Now close your eyes and go to sleep."

Pinocchio closed his eyes and pretended to sleep, while Gepetto melted a little glue in the egg-shell and stuck the feet to the legs; and he joined them so neatly that you couldn't see where it was done. As soon as the marionette saw his new feet fastened on, he jumped down and capered around as if crazy with delight.

"To pay you back for all you have done for me," he said, "please let me start to school right away."

"Good boy!"

"But if I go to school, I must have some clothes to wear."

Gepetto was so poor that he hadn't a cent in his pocket, but he made him a suit out of cardboard, a pair of shoes out of some bark, and a cap out of bread paste. Pinocchio capered off to admire himself in a pan of water, and was so pleased that he strutted up and down saying, "Now I look exactly like a gentleman!"

"Yes, indeed," replied Gepetto. "It is not so much fine clothes but clean ones that make a gentleman."

"By the way," said the marionette, "if I go to school I shall need a spelling-book."

"You are right, but how shall we get it?"

"Easy enough, you can get one at a bookstore."

"And the money?"

"I haven't any."

"Neither have I," said the good man sadly.

Pinocchio grew downcast too at this. Even a boy can understand what it means to be poor.

"Have patience," said Gepetto, suddenly raising his head; and taking his patched coat he left the house on a run. In a very short time he returned with the desired spelling-book, but his coat was gone. The poor man was in his shirt sleeves, although it was snowing outside.

"Where's your coat, father?" asked Pinocchio.

"I sold it."

"Why?"

"Because it made me too warm."

Pinocchio saw through this excuse at once, and having a good heart down in his little wooden body, he threw his arms about Gepetto and kissed him again and again.

9 Pinocchio Sells His Spelling-Book

THE snow-storm having ceased, Pinocchio started forth to school with his new spelling-book under his arm.   On the way a thousand fantastic ideas ran through his little head, and he built a thousand castles in the air, each finer than the last. And this is the way he talked to himself:

"To-day, at school, I must quickly learn how to read. To-morrow, I must learn how to write; and the next day I must learn how to do sums of figures. After that, because of my ability, I shall earn lots of money; and with the very first coins that come into my pocket I shall at once buy a new coat for my father. It shan't be an ordinary coat, but one trimmed with silver and gold, and with diamond buttons. That poor man certainly deserves it; for in order to get me a book to study with, he has sold the very coat off his back—and in this weather, too. I tell you, there are not many such fathers!"

At this moment he suddenly heard the sound of music of a fife and drum company. "Tweedle, tweedle, tweedle!" went the fifes, and "Boom, boom, boom!" went the drums. He stopped to listen. The sound came from the end of a long street which led to an open square near the seashore.

"Where is that beautiful music?" he said. "It's too bad I have to go to school, or else——"

He looked doubtfully down the street. He

must choose for himself whether to go to school, or to follow the music. Finally he said: "To-day I think I shall hear the music, and to-morrow go to school. Any time will do to go to school."

No sooner said than done; and away he went down the street at full speed. The farther he ran the more clearly he heard the fifes and drums —"Tweedle, tweedle, tweedle!" "Boom, boom, boom!" Pretty soon he found himself in an open square filled with people, who were gathered in front of a large wooden building covered with gayly colored signs and pictures.

"What house is this?" he asked a little boy who stood by.

"Read the signs and you'll know," was the reply.

"I would gladly read them, but I haven't learned how to read yet."

"Bright boy, you! Then I will read it for you. It says: 'Grand Theatre of the Marionettes.' "

"How soon does the play begin?"

"Right away."

"How much does it cost to get in?"

"Five cents."

Pinocchio was by this time in a perfect fever of curiosity, and forgetting all his good resolutions he turned shamelessly to the boy and said: "Will you lend me the money until to-morrow?"

"Willingly, if I had it, but to-day I am short of money myself."

"I will sell you my coat for five pennies," said Pinocchio.

"Who wants a coat made of colored cardboard?   If it should rain it would come to pieces."

"What would you give me for my shoes?"

"They are not fit for anything but the fire."

"How much money would you give for my cap?"

"A fine bargain indeed!—a cap made of paste! The rats would be likely to eat it right off my head."

Pinocchio was on nettles.   He was on the point of making a final offer, but he didn't have the courage.   At last he said: "Would you give me five cents for this new spelling-book?"

"I never buy anything like that from other boys," replied the youngster, who had better judgment than the marionette.

"For five cents *I* will buy your spelling-book," said a second-hand dealer who had chanced to hear the conversation.

And the book was sold on the spot. And all this time poor Gepetto stayed at home shivering with cold, because he had sold his coat to buy a spelling-book for his son!

10 The Marionettes
Welcome Pinocchio

WHEN Pinocchio went into the playhouse, something happened which nearly caused a riot.

The curtain was up and the play had already

begun. Two of the actors were then upon the stage, quarreling away—as is usual in marionette plays—and threatening to beat each other with sticks. The audience was laughing loudly at their antics, for they capered around and motioned as naturally as if they had been real people.

All at once one of them ceased speaking, and looking over the audience he pointed toward the end of the room shouting in a stage voice: "Can it be possible—or do I dream? And yet, that boy yonder is Pinocchio!"

"It is indeed he!" cried another, leaping from behind the scenes.

"Pinocchio, Pinocchio!" shouted all the others in a chorus, running upon the stage; "it is our brother Pinocchio—hooray!"

"Come up here, Pinocchio!" called the first speaker. "Come throw your arms around your wooden brothers."

At this affectionate greeting, Pinocchio gave a leap across the backs of the seats, then over the pit and orchestra, and finally landed upon the stage. Then you could hardly imagine the embraces, the kisses, the loving words, and the handclasps which Pinocchio received from that little wooden company of actors. It was indeed a touching sight. But the audience, when they saw that the play was not going on, began to grow impatient and to call, "We want the comedy! Go on with the play!"

It was all breath thrown away, because the puppets, instead of resuming their parts, redoubled their noise and their antics, and taking Pinocchio upon their shoulders they carried him in front of the footlights.

Just then the manager came out. He was a big, ugly fellow who frightened people merely by looking at them. He had shaggy whiskers as black as ink, and so long that they reached the ground, and he trampled upon the ends when he walked. His mouth was as large as an oven, and his eyes like two red lanterns. In his hands, he carried a huge whip made of snakes and foxes' tails, twisted together.

At sight of him all the players stood dumb, not daring to breathe. One could have heard a fly walk across the ceiling.

"Why do you come here and cause trouble in my theatre?" he demanded of Pinocchio in the harsh voice of an ogre with a cold in his head.

"Believe me, most worthy sir, the fault was not mine——"

"Enough of that! We will settle accounts to-night." And he hung Pinocchio upon the wall.

When the play was over, the manager went into the kitchen, where he had dressed a sheep for his dinner and placed it on a spit. But he needed some more wood for the fire to finish roasting it, so he called to two of the puppets:

"Bring me the marionette that you will find hanging yonder on a nail. He appears to be made of nice dry wood and ought to make a splendid fire for finishing this roast."

At first the two puppets hesitated, but a glance from their master's eye made them obey. They soon came back to the kitchen carrying poor Pinocchio who was wriggling like an eel and crying in despair, "Oh, father, save me! I don't want to die! I don't want to die!"

11 Fire-Eater Sneezes and Forgives

THE manager, Fire-Eater (for that was his name), seemed to be a terrible fellow; that is to say, he looked terrible with that shaggy black beard covering his body and legs like an apron. But at heart he was not such a bad man.

When he saw the struggles of poor Pinocchio, and heard his screams, he was touched with pity. For a little while he resisted his feelings, then when he could not hold in any longer he gave forth a tremendous sneeze.

At that sneeze one of the puppets who had carried Pinocchio in, and who had since been doubled up with weeping, began to brighten up, and leaning over he whispered:

"Good news, brother! Our master has sneezed, and that is a sure sign that he is moved with pity for you, and that you are saved."

You must know that when men are sorry they cry or at least rub their eyes. But Fire-Eater was different—he always had to sneeze. That was his way of showing the tenderness of his heart.

After he had sneezed, the showman looked particularly fierce and yelled at Pinocchio: "Stop weeping! Your cries have given me a *very* bad feeling in the pit of my stomach. I feel a spasm that almost—ah, chee! ah, choo!"

"Heaven bless you!" said Pinocchio.[1]

[1] It is customary in Italy and elsewhere to bless one who has sneezed.

"Thanks.   And your father and mother, are they still living?" asked Fire-Eater.

"My father is; but I never had a mother."

"What distress it would have caused your old father, if you had been thrown into the fire. Poor old man, how I pity him! ah, chee! ah, choo! ah, chee!"

"Heaven bless you!" said Pinocchio.

"Thanks.   But then somebody must pity me too, for you see I have no more wood to roast my mutton and, to tell the truth, you would have made a fine blaze.   Now that I have felt pity I must be patient.   Instead of you, I guess I shall have to burn one of the puppets in my company. Come here, guards!"

At this command two wooden officers marched in with caps on their heads and swords at their sides.   Then the showman said to them in a hoarse voice:

"Seize upon Harlequin here and throw him on the fire.   I must have my mutton well roasted."

Think of poor Harlequin's fix!   He was so scared that his legs gave way under him and he fell flat on the ground.   At this sad sight, Pinocchio threw himself at the manager's feet and weeping so hard that he wet the end of the long black whiskers, he cried in a pleading voice: "Have pity, Mr. Fire-Eater!"

"There are no misters here," said the showman in a hard voice.

"Have pity, my lord."

"There are no lords here."

"Have pity, general."

"There are no generals here, either."

"Have pity, your excellency."

When he heard himself called "excellency," the showman at once became softened. He said to Pinocchio in a kindly voice: "Well, what do you want of me?"

"I beg of you to spare poor Harlequin."

"I don't see how I can spare him. I have let you go, and I must have some one to put on the fire, in order to roast my mutton well."

"In that case," said Pinocchio bravely, "in that case I know my duty. Come, sir guards! Tie my hands and throw *me* on the fire. It is not right that my friends should suffer in my stead."

At these words, pronounced in a loud heroic voice, all the puppets began to cry. Even the guards, though made of wood, began to cry like a couple of lambs.

Fire-Eater at first sat silent and unmoved like

a piece of ice.   But at last, little by little, he began to soften and then sneeze.   And after sneez-
ing four or five times he opened his arms to Pinocchio, saying:

"You are indeed a brave boy!   Come and give
me a kiss."

Pinocchio ran to him and climbing his beard
as nimbly as a squirrel gave him a big kiss on the
end of his nose.

"Then am I to be spared too?" asked poor
Harlequin in a frightened little voice.

"Yes," replied Fire-Eater sighing and shaking
his head.   "I must have patience and eat my mutton half roasted this evening.   But woe to the
next one!"

When they learned that everybody was spared,
the puppets ran to the stage, and turning up the
lights, began to frolic and dance as if it were a
gala night.   And they danced until the next
morning.

12 The Fox and the Cat

THE next morning Fire-Eater called Pinocchio
to one side and asked him, "What is your father's
name?"

"Gepetto," replied the boy.

"And what is his business?"

"He is only a poor man."

"Does he earn much?"

"He earns so much that often he hasn't a cent in his pockets. Why, just think, in order to buy me a spelling-book he had to sell the very coat off his back—a coat, too, that was so patched it looked like a crazy-quilt."

"Poor fellow! I am indeed sorry for him. Now here are five gold pieces. Take them to him as quickly as possible, with my compliments."

You may believe that Pinocchio thanked the good showman a thousand times. He embraced every one of the band of players, even the two guards; and with a light heart set out upon the road for home.

However, he had not gone more than a mile or two when whom should he meet but a Fox who was lame in one foot, and a Cat who was blind in both eyes. They were going along as best they could, each helping the other like good comrades. The Fox, since he was lame, leaned upon the Cat's shoulder; and the Cat, since he was blind, was guided by the Fox.

"Good-morning, Pinocchio," said the Fox bowing politely.

"How did you come to know my name?" asked the marionette.

"I know your father well."

"Where have you seen him?"

"I saw him yesterday in the doorway of his home."

"What was he doing?"

"He was in his shirt-sleeves and shivered from the cold."

"Poor father! But, heaven willing, he shan't shiver any more after to-day."

"Why?"

"Because I have become a rich lord."

"You a rich lord!" said the Fox laughing sneeringly. The Cat laughed also, but in order to hide it he brushed his moustache with his paw.

"There is nothing to laugh at," said Pinocchio in a huff. "I don't want to make you feel envious, but look at these beautiful gold pieces."

And he pulled out of his pocket the money that Fire-Eater had given him. At the pleasing jingle of the gold, the Fox forgot himself so far as to straighten out his lame leg, while the Cat opened wide both his eyes which looked like two green lanterns, but closed them again so quickly that Pinocchio did not notice them.

"What are you going to do with all this money?" asked the Fox.

"First of all," answered Pinocchio, "I am going to buy for my father a fine new coat trimmed with gold and silver and with diamond buttons. Then I shall buy a spelling-book for myself."

"For yourself?"

"Why not? I intend to go to school and study and be a good boy."

"Look at me," said the Fox. "On account of my foolish passion for study I lost the use of one leg."

"Look at me," said the Cat. "On account of my foolish passion for study I lost the sight of both eyes."

Just then a blackbird, sitting on a fence by the road, called out warningly, "Pinocchio, do not heed the advice of bad companions. If you do you will rue it."

The words were hardly out of the bird's mouth when the Cat gave a sudden spring and caught him, and without giving him even time to say "Oh!" he ate him at a mouthful, feathers and all. When he had finished the Cat washed his face, shut his eyes again, and became as blind as ever.

"Poor bird!" said Pinocchio to the Cat; "why did you treat him so badly?"

"To teach him a lesson. Another time he will know better than to meddle with other folks' affairs."

The three walked along together for a short distance when the Fox, stopping suddenly, said: "Would you like to double your money?"

"What do you mean?"

"Would you like, instead of five paltry little gold pieces, to have a hundred or a thousand?"

"Wouldn't I though! But how could it be done?"

"Easy enough. Instead of going home at once, come along with us."

"Where do you want to take me?"

"To the Owl Country."[1]

Pinocchio thought about it a little while and then said resolutely: "No, I can't go with you. I am not far away from home now, and my father is looking for me. Who knows if the poor man has not been worried by my absence. The Talking Cricket was right when he warned me against doing my own way. No later than last night I

[1] A phrase meaning also "Foolish Land."

was in dire danger in the Fire-Eater's house. Brrr! it makes me shiver to think of it."

"Then you are determined to go home, eh?" said the Fox. "Go ahead, but it will be so much the worse for you."

"So much the worse for you," repeated the Cat.

"Think it over well, Pinocchio, for you are throwing away a fortune."

"Yes, a fortune," said the Cat.

"Your five gold pieces ought to become two thousand by to-morrow."

"Two thousand," repeated the Cat.

"But how could they possibly become so many?" asked Pinocchio standing with his mouth open.

"I will tell you," said the Fox. "You must know that in the Owl Country there is a magic piece of ground called the Wonder Field. You go to this field and dig a little hole and bury, say, one of your gold pieces. Then you fill up the hole and sprinkle a few drops of water over it, also a little salt, and go to bed and sleep soundly. During the night the gold piece will begin to sprout and blossom, and the next morning when you get up and go back to the field, what do you find?   Why, you find a beautiful tree as full of gold pieces as an ear of corn is of kernels."

"How would it be," said Pinocchio, very much excited, "if I should bury all five of the gold pieces?"

"That is easy to count up," replied the Fox; "you can do it on your fingers.   For each piece you will make five hundred; and so for five pieces you ought to get two thousand five hundred."

"Oh, how beautiful!" cried Pinocchio dancing with delight.   "As soon as I make all those, I will keep two thousand for myself, and give you five hundred as a present."

"Give us a *present?*" said the Fox greatly offended.   "Not by any means!"

"Not by any means!" repeated the Cat.

"As for us," continued the Fox, "we do not work for selfish ends.   We work only to enrich others."

"Enrich others," repeated the Cat.

"What noble people!" thought Pinocchio to himself; and forgetting all about his good resolutions, his father, the new coat, and the rest, he said to the Fox and the Cat:

"Come along—I'm with you!"

13 The Red Lobster Inn

THEY walked and walked and walked until toward nightfall, when they came to the Red Lobster Inn. Pinocchio felt that he couldn't go a step farther.

"Let's stop here awhile," said the Fox, "for a

little supper and rest.   At midnight we can start
again and by morning we will reach the Wonder
Field."

So they went in and seated themselves around
a table; but nobody seemed hungry. The poor
Cat had stomach trouble and couldn't eat anything except thirty-five small fish with tomato
sauce, and four helpings of tripe; and because the
tripe was not well seasoned he had to help it down
with three portions of butter and grated cheese.

The Fox would have been glad to order something, but his doctor had ordered a strict diet for
him. He had to content himself with a tender
young rabbit dressed with chicken giblets. After
the rabbit he topped off with a few partridges,
pheasants, frogs, lizards, and some grapes. That
was all he could eat. The very sight of food, he
said, was distasteful to him, and he didn't want
another mouthful.

Pinocchio ate the least of all.   He ordered a
slice of meat and bread and left most of it on his
plate.   He was so occupied with thoughts of the
Wonder Field that he couldn't think of anything
else.

Supper over, the Fox said to the innkeeper:
"Give us two good rooms, one for Mr. Pinocchio,

and the other for my friend and myself. We will take a little nap before starting. But remember to call us at midnight sharp so that we may continue our journey."

"Very good, sir," said the innkeeper winking at the Fox and the Cat, as if to say, "We understand each other."

As soon as Pinocchio went to bed he fell asleep and began to dream. He dreamed that he was in the midst of a field full of little trees, and these trees were loaded with gold pieces, and every time the wind shook them they went *"Tinkle, tinkle, tinkle!"* as if to say, "If you want me, come and get me." But just as Pinocchio was reaching for them in order to fill his pockets, he was awakened by a loud rapping upon his door. It was the innkeeper who came in to say that the hour was midnight.

"Are my companions ready?" asked the marionette.

"Ready? Why they left two hours ago."

"Why were they in such a hurry?"

"The Cat received word that his oldest kitten had frozen his feet and was in grave danger."

"Did they pay for their supper?"

"What a question! Those two good people

are too well-bred to have offered such an affront to your lordship."

"That's too bad! Such an affront would not have displeased me much," said Pinocchio scratching his head. Then he asked, "Where did my good friends say they would meet me?"

"At the Wonder Field, to-morrow morning at daybreak."

Pinocchio paid one of his gold pieces for the supper of himself and his friends and then set forth. But outside the inn it was so dark that he could not see the way; he went stumbling along. The country on all sides was so quiet that you couldn't hear a leaf stir. Some bats came flying across the road and struck Pinocchio on the nose, so that he jumped with fright and cried out:

"Who's there?" and from the distant hills came back the echo, "Who's there? Who's there? Who's there?"

He walked on a little farther and saw on the trunk of a tree a small creature that shone with a pale dim light like a wax candle behind a ground glass shade.

"Who are you?" asked Pinocchio.

"I am the ghost of the Talking Cricket," answered the creature in a far-away voice which seemed to come from another world.

"What do you want?"

"I want to give you some advice. Go back at once to your father with the four gold pieces you have left. He is in deep sorrow because he thinks you are lost."

"To-morrow my father will be a very rich man, because these four pieces will have become two thousand."

"My boy, do not trust any one who promises to make you rich over night. They are either fools or knaves. Listen to me and go back."

"But I want to go on."

"The hour is late."

"I want to go on."

"The night is dark."

"I want to go on."

"The road is dangerous."

"I want to go on."

"Remember—boys who insist upon doing as they please are sorry for it sooner or later."

"The same old story. Good-night Cricket."

"Good-night, Pinocchio, and may heaven keep you out of the hands of thieves."

With that the Talking Cricket disappeared, just like some one had blown out a candle, and the road seemed darker than ever.

14 Pinocchio Falls among Thieves

"TRULY," said the marionette starting again on his way, "how unlucky we poor boys are! Everybody scolds us, everybody warns us, everybody gives us advice. If you listen to anybody they at once try to lord it over you like a father or a teacher. Look at that bore of a Talking Cricket: Because I don't follow all his advice he tells me all sorts of things will happen. He says I will meet with thieves! Now I've never believed in thieves. I think they are only a bugaboo that our fathers make up to keep us in of nights. Suppose I *should* meet them—do you think I'd be scared? Not in the least! I'd walk right up to them and I'd say: 'Sir thieves, what do you want of me? I will have no trifling! So go along and mind your own business!' and at hearing talk like that the cowardly thieves would scamper away like the wind. And if they were wise enough to scamper one way, I would scamper the other—and that would end the matter."

But Pinocchio did not have time to end his reasoning, for just then he fancied he heard a slight rustling of leaves behind him. He turned sharply and made out two coal-black figures covered with black sacks and hopping along on tiptoe like a couple of ghosts.

"Here they are, for a fact!" said Pinocchio to himself; and not knowing where to hide the four gold pieces he clapped them in his mouth. Then he tried to run away, but had hardly gone a step before he was seized by the arms and he heard two gruff, cavernous voices call out:

"Your money or your life!"

Pinocchio was not able to reply on account of having the money in his mouth; so he made a thousand bows and grimaces in order to let the robbers know that he was only a poor marionette who didn't have a cent to his name.

"Come, come, out with it!   Stop your fooling!" commanded one of the thieves.

The captive only made signs with his head and hands, as if to say, "I haven't any."

"Out with it, I say, or you're a dead one!" said the taller of the two thieves.

"You're a dead one!" repeated the other.

"And when we've finished you, we'll get your father too."

"We'll get your father too," repeated the other.

"No, no, no—not my poor father!" cried Pinocchio in terror; but as he spoke the gold pieces jingled in his mouth.

"Oh, you rascal!   You have hidden that money under your tongue.   Spit it out!"

Pinocchio didn't budge.

"Ah, now you pretend to be deaf! Just wait a little and we'll make you give it up!"

So saying they began to maltreat the poor boy. The taller one took him by the nose and began to choke him, to force his mouth open, but could not manage it. Then the shorter one tried to force a knife between his teeth, when Pinocchio, quick as lightning caught the fellow's hand between his teeth. Fancy his surprise when he found that it was not a man's hand, but only the paw of a cat!

Encouraged by this first victory, Pinocchio gave a sudden twist and freed himself from the thieves' clutches, and jumping a fence at the side of the road he started across country at full speed—the thieves after him like two dogs after a rabbit.

After running several miles Pinocchio had to stop. Thinking himself lost, he climbed to the top of a tall pine tree and sat down to rest. The thieves soon arrived and tried to climb up after him; but when they got halfway they slipped back to the ground skinning their hands and feet.

But they were not ready to give up. On the contrary, they collected a bunch of dry wood, piled it up at the foot of the tree and set fire to it.

In less time than I can tell it, the pine flared up like a huge wind-blown torch. Pinocchio saw the flames growing larger, and not wishing to be finished like a broiled pigeon he gave a great leap from the tree-top to the ground, and began to run again across the fields and vineyards. And the thieves were right on his heels!

Presently the morning began to dawn, and Pinocchio discovered, right across his path, a great deep ditch full of muddy water the color of coffee and milk. What was to be done? "One, two, three!" counted the marionette and with a tremendous jump he landed on the other side. The two thieves tried to leap after him but their feet slipped and *kersplash!* they went right into the middle of the ditch.

Pinocchio heard the splash, and laughed, and called out: "A fine bath, sir thieves!"

For a moment he thought they were drowned, but looking back he saw that they had scrambled across and were after him, still wrapped in their sacks from which the water poured in a steady stream.

15 The Thieves Hang Pinocchio

THEN the marionette began to lose heart. He was on the point of throwing himself upon the ground and giving up, when he saw far off, in the middle of the forest, a little cottage white and glistening as snow.

"If I can only manage to reach that cottage, I shall be saved," he said to himself.

And without losing a moment he ran on through the forest as hard as he could, the thieves close after him. After a desperate chase of two hours he came, out of breath, to the door of the cottage and knocked. No one answered.

Again he knocked, louder, for the sound of running feet and heavy breathing told him that the pursuers were almost upon him.

Still no reply.

Seeing that knocking would have no effect, Pinocchio began to kick desperately upon the door. Then a window opened and there appeared a beautiful Fairy with blue hair and pale face like a figure of wax. Her eyes were closed and her hands were folded. Without moving her lips she said in a far-away voice which seemed to come from another world:

"No one lives here; all gone away."

"Open the door!" cried Pinocchio pleadingly.

"I also have gone away."

Saying this, the Fairy disappeared and the window closed without the least noise.

"Oh, beautiful Fairy with the Blue Hair," cried Pinocchio, "open to me, for pity's sake. Have compassion upon a poor boy pursued by thieves——"

But before he could finish he felt himself seized by the collar, and heard two rough voices growling out, "Now you shall not get away again!"

The marionette, sure that his end had come, shook and trembled in every joint until he fairly rattled; so did the four gold pieces still hidden under his tongue.

"Now will you open your mouth or not?" demanded the thieves. "Ah! you won't reply? Very well—this time we'll *make* you open it!"

They drew out two knives as sharp as razors, and *whack, whack!* they gave him two hard slashes across the back. But fortunately the marionette was made of the hardest wood. The knife blades broke all to pieces, leaving only the handles in the hands of the robbers.

"I see we'll have to hang him," said one to the other. "That's the ticket!"

"That's the ticket!" repeated the other.

No sooner said than done. They tied his hands together, and slipping a rope around his neck they strung him up to the limb of a huge tree

called the Great Oak.   Then they calmly sat down
upon the grass and waited for him to die. But
after three hours the marionette's eyes were still
open, his mouth was closed, and he kicked harder
than ever.

After a while they got tired of waiting, and
turned to Pinocchio saying mockingly: "Good-
bye until to-morrow. We will return then, and
hope you will be polite enough to open your
mouth for us."

Thereupon they went away.

After a while a great wind arose and blew the
marionette back and forth like the clapper of a
bell. It made the rope tighten until he could
scarcely breathe. He feared that he must soon
die, but still hoped that some one would come
and rescue him. All in vain. No one came and
he felt himself growing weaker. Then he be-
thought himself of his poor father, and murmured:

"Oh, my father! If you were only here!"

At last his breath failed him and he hung silent.

16 The Fairy with
the Blue Hair

WHILE poor Pinocchio hung from the limb of
the Great Oak, seemingly more dead than alive,
the Fairy with the Blue Hair came again to the

window.   At sight of the unhappy boy swinging backward and forward in the wind, she was moved with pity.   She clapped her hands three times, and at this signal the flutter of wings was heard and a great Falcon came and alighted upon the window ledge.

"What are your commands, my gracious Fairy?" he asked bowing low.   For you must know that the Fairy with the Blue Hair was none other than a good spirit who had lived near this forest for a thousand years.

"Do you see that marionette hanging to a limb of the Great Oak?"

"Yes."

"Then fly quickly and cut with your strong beak the rope that chokes him, lay him gently on the ground, and then come back to me."

In two minutes the Falcon flew back, saying: "I have done as you commanded."

"And how did you find him—alive or dead?"

"From his looks I thought him dead, but he cannot be entirely so, because the moment I cut the knot which held him, he gave a sigh and murmured: 'Ah, I feel better!'"

Then the Fairy clapped her hands twice and there appeared a fine-looking Dog walking along on his hind legs just like a man. He was dressed in full coachman's livery. He wore a cap trimmed in gold lace and under it a light curly wig. His coat was of chocolate color, set off by diamond buttons and provided with two large pockets in which to stow away bones. His trousers were of rich crimson velvet, and he had silk stockings and low shoes. Behind him he carried a sort of umbrella case of blue satin in which to thrust his tail when the weather was stormy.

"My good Rover," said the Fairy, "run quickly and harness up the finest coach in my stables, and then drive into the forest. When you come to the Great Oak you will find upon the ground a poor little marionette, half dead. Take him up carefully and bring him here to me. Do you understand?"

The Dog wagged his tail three or four times to show that he understood, and was off like a shot. It was not long until there came out from the stables a handsome sky-blue carriage all tufted inside with canary bird feathers the color of whipped cream. It was drawn by a hundred pairs of white mice, and the Dog sat up on the box cracking his whip from right to left in great style.

A quarter of an hour had scarcely gone by when the carriage returned, and the Fairy who had waited at the door took the marionette in her arms and carried him to a bed inlaid with mother-of-pearl, and sent at once for the most famous doctors of that neighborhood.

One after another the doctors arrived. They were a Crow, a Screech-Owl, and a Talking Cricket.

"Gentlemen," said the Fairy, "I should like to know whether this marionette is alive or dead."

At this question, the Crow came forward first, felt the patient's pulse, looked in his nose, tickled him on the feet, and after this examination gave the following solemn opinion:

"It is my belief that the patient is dead; but if through some oversight he should not be dead, then it would be a sure sign that he is still alive."

"It grieves me," said the Owl, "to have to contradict the Crow, my illustrious friend and colleague. It is my belief that the patient is alive; but if through some oversight he should not be alive, then it would be a sure sign that he is dead."

"And have you nothing to say?" asked the Fairy of the Talking Cricket.

"I say that the prudent doctor always keeps

silent when he doesn't understand a case. For the rest, the marionette's face looks familiar to me. I have known him for some time."

Pinocchio, who up to that time had been lying as stiff as a stick of wood, now gave such a start that he shook the whole bed.

"This marionette," continued the Cricket, "is a sorry rascal."

Pinocchio opened his eyes and shut them quickly.

"He is a scamp, a rogue, a vagabond."

Pinocchio hid his head under the coverlet.

"This marionette is a disobedient son who is likely to break his poor father's heart."

At this point the sound of weeping could be heard. Just imagine how surprised they all were when, lifting the coverlet, they found that the noise came from Pinocchio!

"When a dead boy cries," said the Crow solemnly, "it is a sure sign that he is getting well."

"It grieves me to contradict my illustrious friend and colleague," said the Owl; "but it seems to me that when a live boy cries, it is a sure sign that he doesn't want to die."

17 Pinocchio Gets Well—
And Tells a Lie

WHEN the three doctors had gone, the Fairy came
to Pinocchio and, upon touching his forehead,
perceived that he had a high fever. So she put a

white powder in a glass of water and gave it to him, saying gently:

"Drink this and after a while you will be well."

Pinocchio gazed at the glass, made a wry face, and asked whiningly:

"Is it sweet or bitter?"

"It is bitter but will do you good."

"If it is bitter, I don't want it."

"Listen to me; drink it."

"But I don't like bitter things."

"Drink it, and then I will give you a lump of sugar to take the taste out of your mouth."

"Where is the lump of sugar?"

"Here it is."

"Give it to me first, and then I will take the medicine."

"You promise?"

"Yes."

The Fairy gave him the sugar, and Pinocchio soon finished it; then he said, licking his lips, "How nice it would be if sugar were medicine! I'd take it every day."

"Now keep your promise and take the medicine," said the Fairy; "it will make you well."

Pinocchio held the glass in his hand and sniffed

at its contents; then put it to his mouth; then smelled it again; and finally said:

"It's too bitter—too bitter! I can't possibly gulp it down."

"How can you say that when you haven't tasted it?"

"Oh, I can imagine—I can tell by the smell! Give me another lump of sugar and then I will drink it."

So the Fairy, with all the patience of an indulgent mamma, put another lump of sugar in his mouth and then handed him the medicine again.

"Truly I can't drink it!" wailed the marionette with a thousand grimaces.

"Why?"

"Because that pillow is too close to my feet."

The Fairy moved the pillow.

"It's no use—I can't drink it."

"What else annoys you?"

"That door is ajar."

The Fairy shut the door.

"Honestly, I can't drink that bitter stuff," howled Pinocchio. "No, no, no!"

"My boy, you will be sorry."

"I don't care."

"You'll die of the fever."

"I don't care. I'd rather die than take that bitter medicine."

"All right, then," said the Fairy.

At this the door opened and in walked four Rabbits, black as ink, and carrying a coffin on their shoulders.

"What do you want?" cried Pinocchio sitting up.

"We have come to take you away," said the largest Rabbit.

"To take me away? Why, I'm not dead yet!"

"No, not yet; but you will be in a few moments since you have refused the medicine that would make you well."

"O my Fairy, my Fairy!" yelled Pinocchio, "give me that medicine—quickly! Send them away—I don't want to die—I don't want to die!"

And he seized the glass with both hands and drank the dose down at one gulp.

"Pshaw!" said the Rabbits, "we have come on a fool's errand." And taking the coffin up on their shoulders they went away grumbling.

Not long afterward Pinocchio jumped out of bed entirely well; for, you must know, that wooden boys are rarely ill and then get well quickly. When the Fairy saw him capering around the room happy as a chicken that has just burst its shell, she said:

"So my medicine has really cured you?"

"Yes, indeed. I had a close call."

"Then why did you make such a fuss about taking it?"

"Oh, boys are all alike. We are more afraid of the medicine than of the illness."

"For shame! Boys ought to know that a good remedy taken in time often keeps off a dangerous sickness—perhaps death."

"The next time I shan't be so bad. I shall remember those black Rabbits and the coffin—then I'll take the medicine right away."

"That's right. Now come and tell me how you happened to fall into the hands of thieves."

Pinocchio told faithfully all that had happened to him. When he had ended, the Fairy asked:

"What did you do with the four gold pieces?"

"I lost them," replied Pinocchio; but he told a lie, because he had them in his pocket.

The moment he said this, his nose, which was already long enough, grew four inches longer.

"Where did you lose them?" asked the Fairy.

"In the forest near here."

At this second lie, the nose grew still longer.

"If you have lost them in the forest near here," said the Fairy, "we shall soon find them; for everything here is always found."

"Ah, now I recollect," said the marionette. "I did not lose the coins, but I swallowed them when I took the medicine."

At the third lie, Pinocchio's nose grew so long that he couldn't turn around. If he turned one way he struck it against the bedpost or the window. If he turned the other, he hit the wall or the door.

The Fairy looked at him and began to laugh.

"Why are you laughing?" asked the marionette sheepishly.

"I laugh at the foolish lies you have told."

"How did you know they were lies?"

"Lies, my boy, are recognized at once, because they are of only two kinds. Some have short legs, and others have long noses. Yours are the kind that have long noses."

Pinocchio was so crestfallen that he tried to run away and hide himself, but he couldn't. His nose had grown so long that he couldn't get it through the door.

18 The Fox
and the Cat Again

THE Fairy let the marionette cry and howl for a
good half hour on account of his long nose. She
did this in order to teach him a lesson upon the

folly of telling falsehoods.   But when she saw his
eyes swollen and his face red with weeping, she
was moved by pity for him.   She clapped her
hands together, and at the signal a large flock of
woodpeckers flew into the window and, alighting
one by one upon Pinocchio's nose, they pecked
so hard that in a few moments it was reduced to
its usual size.

"How good you are, dear Fairy!" said the
marionette wiping his eyes; "and how I love
you!"

"I love you too," replied the Fairy, "and if you
would like to live here in my house you shall be
my little brother."

"I would do so gladly—but my poor
father——?"

"I have arranged all that.   Your father has
been told already, and will join us here before
nightfall."

"Truly?" cried Pinocchio dancing around
with delight.   "Then, my Fairy, if you will let
me I would like to go and meet him.   I can hardly
wait to see the dear old man who has suffered
so much for me."

"Go, then, but be careful not to lose your way.

Take the road to the forest and you will surely meet him."

Pinocchio set forth, and as soon as he was in the forest he began to run like a deer. But when he reached a certain spot opposite the Great Oak he stopped, thinking that he heard some one. In fact he saw coming along the road—whom do you suppose?—why, the Fox and the Cat, the same two persons who had supped with him at the Red Lobster Inn.

"Well, if here isn't our dear Pinocchio!" cried the Fox running up to him and throwing both arms around his neck. "How did you ever get here?"

"How did you ever get here?" repeated the Cat.

"It's a long story," said the marionette, "which I shall have to tell you later. Do you know, the other night after you had left me at the Inn I met two thieves on the highway."

"Two thieves? Oh, my poor friend! And what did they want?"

"They tried to rob me of my money."

"Infamous!" said the Fox.

"Most infamous!" said the Cat.

"But I got away from them," continued the marionette; "then they pursued me and after a long chase they caught me and hung me upon a limb of that oak tree yonder."

"Who ever heard of such a thing!" said the Fox. "What a world we live in, where nobody can be safe any more!"

While they were talking, Pinocchio noticed that one of the Cat's paws was tied up as if it were hurt.

"What's the matter with your paw?" he asked.

The Cat tried to answer but grew confused, so the Fox said for him: "My friend is so modest he doesn't like to talk. He got his foot hurt through mistaken kindness to a Wolf. My friend has such a kind heart!" and the Fox wiped away a tear.

Pinocchio also was very much touched by this. "Never mind!" he said patting the Cat on the shoulder.

"Where are you going now?" asked the Fox of Pinocchio.

"I am on my way to meet my father, who may arrive here at any moment."

"And your money?"

"Oh, I have that safe enough in my pocket, all except the coin I spent at the Red Lobster."

"And to think that those four gold pieces could so easily become a thousand or two by to-morrow! Why don't you follow my advice and plant them in the Wonder Field?"

"To-day it is impossible. Some other day we might do it."

"Some other day will be too late," said the Fox.

"Why?"

"Because this land has just been bought by a rich lord, and after to-morrow nobody will be permitted to plant things in it."

"How far away is it?"

"Not more than two miles. Will you come along now? In half an hour you'll be there. Then you can plant your coins at once, and in a few minutes you can harvest your two thousand, and this evening you'll have your pockets full. Will you come?"

Pinocchio hesitated. He remembered the advice of the good Fairy, and of old Gepetto, and of the Talking Cricket. But he ended by doing like all silly little boys who want to please themselves. With a nod of his head he said to the Fox and Cat, "All right, I'm with you!" and they started.

After walking for about half a day they came to a city called "Fools-Trap." When they had entered it Pinocchio saw in every street lean dogs yawning with hunger, shorn sheep which trembled from cold, plucked chickens which gaped for aid, butterflies without wings, peacocks whose tails had been cut off, and other forlorn animals.

In the midst of this wretched throng they passed, from time to time, fine carriages whose occupants proved to be some Fox or Magpie or Vulture.

"Where is the Wonder Field?" demanded Pinocchio.

"Only a few steps farther."

In proof of this they went on through the city and stopped outside the walls in a deserted field that looked like other fields.

"Here we are," said the Fox; "now just stoop down, dig a little hole with your hands, and plant your gold pieces."

Pinocchio obeyed. He dug a hole and put the four coins in it, then covered it all over again.

"Now then," said the Fox, "bring a little water

from that ditch and sprinkle over the place where you have planted the gold."

Pinocchio went to the ditch, and as he had no bucket he took off one of his shoes, filled it with water, and sprinkled the ground. Then he asked:

"Is there anything else to do?"

"Nothing else," replied the Fox. "Now we can go away. In twenty minutes you can come back and find a little tree sprouting up, with all its branches full of gold pieces."

The silly marionette, almost crazy with joy at the prospect, thanked the Fox and Cat a thousand times and promised them a splendid gift.

"We don't wish anything," they replied. "We are satisfied to have taught you how to get rich without labor; it is our best reward."

With this they bade farewell to Pinocchio, wished him a fine harvest, and went their way.

19 Pinocchio Is Thrown into Prison

THE marionette went back to the city and began to count the minutes one by one; and as soon as he thought the time was up he returned hastily to the Wonder Field. As he walked along with impatient steps his heart beat like a clock, *tick— tock, tick—tock!* and he was thinking to himself:

"What if I should find five thousand gold pieces instead of two thousand? What if I should find a hundred thousand? Oh, what a rich man I should be! I would have a fine palace, and a stable full of horses and carriages; and I would have a cellar full of sweetmeats and a pantry full of cakes and candies."

With such wild dreams as these he finally reached the field and began to look for the tree laden with gold; but saw nothing. He went a hundred steps further; nothing. He went all around the field until he reached the hole where he had planted his money; and still nothing. He took off his hat and scratched his head in perplexity.

Just then he heard a burst of laughter, and looking upward he saw a large Parrot who was cleaning his feathers with his bill.

"What are you laughing at?" asked Pinocchio in a rage.

"I laugh because in preening my wings I tickled myself."

The marionette had no reply for this. He went again to the ditch and filling his shoe with water as before, sprinkled the earth above his treasure,—when behold, another peal of laughter more impertinent than the first echoed through the silent field!

"Vulgar fellow, do you know what you are laughing about now?" cried Pinocchio wrathfully.

"I laugh at those simpletons who believe every tomfoolery that is told them and who fall into every trap."

"Do you mean me?"

"Yes, I mean you, Pinocchio. You are foolish enough to believe that money grows like corn. I thought so too, once upon a time, but I suffered for it. Now—too late!—I have found out that in order to gain money honestly one must work either with his hands or with his head."

"I don't understand you," said the marionette, who began to tremble with fear.

"Then I will explain myself," said the Parrot. "Know then, that while you were away in the city, the Fox and the Cat came back here and stole your money and fled like the wind. You'll never be able to catch them."

Pinocchio stood with open mouth; and not wishing to believe the Parrot's story he com-

menced to dig up the ground with his fingers.   He
dug and dug and dug until he had made a hole
so large that a haystack might be put in it.   But
he never found a trace of the money.

Then in despair he returned to the city.   He
went into the court of law to lodge a complaint
against the robbers who had stolen his money.

The Judge was a Monkey of the race of Goril-
las.   He was very old and looked dignified on
account of his white beard and gold eye-glasses,
without lenses, which he wore all the time on account of weak eyes.

Pinocchio told the Judge all about the fraud
which had been practiced upon him, and gave
the names and descriptions of the thieves.   He
ended by asking for justice.

The Judge listened to him with a kind face and
seemed greatly interested and even moved. When
the marionette had finished his story he stretched
out his hand and rang a bell.   At this summons
two Mastiffs dressed like policemen entered the
room.

Then the Judge pointed at Pinocchio and said,
"This silly fellow has been robbed of all his
money.   Arrest him and put him in prison."

The marionette on hearing this sentence could

hardly believe his ears. Then he began to protest; but the officers, in order to avoid a useless waste of time, clapped him over the mouth and put him in a prison-cell.

And there he had to stay for four long months —and probably would have been there much longer if it had not been for a lucky happening. It seems that the Emperor of the city of Fools-Trap won a victory over his enemies, and to celebrate it he ordered a great festival with fireworks, parades and feasts; and in order to make still greater rejoicing he opened all the prisons and set the criminals at liberty.

"If the other prisoners are freed, I ought to be too," said Pinocchio to the jailer.

"You?—no," replied the jailer; "you are not an evil-doer."

"Excuse me," replied Pinocchio, "but if it comes to that I'm as bad as any of them."

"Then you are right," said the jailer; and taking off his hat respectfully he opened the cell door and stood aside with a bow, for the marionette to pass out.

20 A Terrible Serpent

JUST imagine Pinocchio's delight when he was
set free! He did not stop to look back but set out
on a run until he had left the ill-fated city behind

him.   Then he took the road which led to the Fairy's cottage.

There had been a good deal of rain, and the roads were so muddy that he sank in almost to his knees.   But Pinocchio was not to be held back. Eager to see his father again and the Fairy with the Blue Hair, he leaped along like a hunting dog and splashed mud all over himself.   And as he went he said to himself:

"How unlucky I have been!   But I deserved it—I've wanted to do things my own way and haven't listened to advice.   Well, I have learned my lesson and shall do better after this.   How glad I shall be to see my father!   And the Fairy— will she forgive me, I wonder?"

Just then he stopped suddenly in great alarm, and jumped back four steps.

What had he seen?

He had seen a great Serpent lying across the road.   It had a green skin, eyes of flame, and its sharp tail smoked like a chimney.

It would be impossible to picture the marionette's fear.   Back he ran and seated himself upon a pile of stones, waiting for the Serpent to go on his way and leave the road clear.

He waited an hour—two hours—three hours

—but the Serpent didn't budge. Finally Pinocchio plucked up courage, came up toward the Serpent and said in a soft, polite voice:

"I—I beg your pardon, Mr. Serpent, but would you do me the favor to draw over to one side a little, so that I may get by you?"

He might as well have talked to a wall. There was no reply. The marionette continued in the same voice:

"You must know, Mr. Serpent, that I am going home to see my father, after a long time; so please let me pass."

Still no answer. But the Serpent who up to that time had been full of life now grew motionless and stiff. His eyes closed and his tail ceased to smoke.

"I wonder if he is dead?" said Pinocchio rubbing his hands with relief. And without further delay he started to jump over. But he had no more than lifted one leg when the Serpent rose suddenly like a Jack-in-the-box. The marionette tried to jump back but lost his balance and landed in a mud-hole, head first, and feet kicking wildly in air.

At this sight the Serpent was seized with such a fit of laughter, that he couldn't stop. He laughed and laughed until he choked himself. And this time he was really dead.

Pinocchio now plucked up courage and started again on his way to the Fairy's cottage. He ran and ran for a long while. But the road was so long and muddy that he could hardly travel. Besides he was gnawed by a terrible hunger.

At last he jumped over a fence into a field with the intention of picking a few grapes; but again ill fortune awaited him. He had no sooner reached the vine than *crack!* he felt his foot seized by teeth of iron which made him see all the stars in the heavens. The poor marionette was fast in a trap!

21 Pinocchio Plays
Watch-Dog

PINOCCHIO lifted up his voice in a great outcry;
but his cries and screams were useless, as there
were no houses near by, and no people on the
highway.

Night drew on. On account of the pain of the trap, and his fear at being alone in this dark, silent field, the marionette nearly fainted. Just then a Fire-fly passed over his head and he called to it:

"Oh, little Fire-fly, would you have the kindness to free me from this torture?"

"Poor little boy!" replied the Fire-fly regarding him with pity. "How did you come to get caught in that trap?"

"I came into the field to pick a few grapes and——"

"But were the grapes yours?"

"No."

"Then who taught you to take other people's grapes?"

"I was hungry."

"Hunger, my boy, is no excuse."

"I know it," wailed Pinocchio; "I wouldn't do it, next time."

At this moment they heard steps approaching. It was the farmer who owned the field coming quietly to see if he had caught one of the thieving weasels that had been eating his chickens. Great was his astonishment to see, by the light of his dark lantern, that he had caught a boy instead of a weasel.

"Ah, you little rascal!" he shouted angrily: "so it's you that carries off my chickens?"

"No, no, not I!" sobbed Pinocchio. "I came into the field only to get a bunch or two of grapes."

"He who steals grapes is quite likely to steal chickens too. Leave it to me. I'll give you a lesson you'll remember for a while."

He opened the trap and took the marionette out by the back of the neck like a kitten, and carried him to the house. When he reached there he said: "It is late and I'm going to bed. We will settle matters to-morrow. Meanwhile, as my watch-dog died to-day I will put you in his place."

With this, he took a big collar all covered with brass nails, and placed it around Pinocchio's neck and secured it so tightly that he couldn't get it off. To the collar was attached a long iron chain which was riveted, at the other end, in the wall.

"If it should happen to rain," said the farmer, "you can crawl into this dog-house and lie down on the straw. It has been my poor dog's bed for four years. But remember—if the thieves come into the yard you are to keep a sharp lookout."

With this warning, the farmer went into his own house and shut and bolted the door; while poor Pinocchio crouched down more dead than alive from fear and cold and hunger. From time to time he tried to ease his collar with his hands saying with a moan:

"It serves me right! It certainly serves me right! But who would have thought that I should end my days living in a dog house and guarding a chicken-coop!"

With these sad thoughts he went into the dog-house and soon fell asleep.

22 And Catches the Thieves

AFTER Pinocchio had slept soundly for more than two hours, he was awakened about midnight by the sound of whispering and voices saying *"Hist,*

hist!" which seemed to come from the barnyard. Thrusting the end of his nose out of the door he saw four animals with mottled coats, something like cats. But they were not cats. They were Weasels—bloodthirsty animals fond of eggs and young chickens. One of the number now approached the dog-house and said in a low voice:

"Good-evening, Rover."

"I'm not Rover," replied the marionette.

"Who are you, then?"

"I am Pinocchio."

"What are you doing here?"

"Playing watch-dog."

"Where is Rover—the old dog who formerly lived here?"

"He died this morning."

"Dead?—poor fellow! He was a good dog. But judging from your looks you are a good dog too."

"I beg your pardon—I'm not a dog."

"What are you then?"

"I'm a marionette."

"And you're just playing watch-dog?"

"Yes—by way of punishment."

"Well, I should like to make the same agreement with you that we had with Rover."

"What is that?" asked Pinocchio.

"We will come here once a week, as we have in the past," said the Weasel, "and carry off eight chickens. Seven of them we shall eat, and one we shall give to you on condition, remember, that you pretend to sleep and do not give any alarm."

"And did Rover do that?"

"Yes, indeed, and the plan worked finely. Now go to sleep and rest assured that upon leaving we will give you a nice fat chicken for your breakfast. Do you understand?"

"Only too well!" replied Pinocchio, with a nod as much as to say, "I'll see you later!"

When the four Weasels felt that they were safe, they crept one by one to the hen-house, opened the little wooden door with their teeth, and slipped inside. But no sooner had they got in than they heard the door slam shut with a bang.

It was Pinocchio who had closed the door, and not content with that he rolled a big stone up against it to keep it shut. Then he began to bark, *"Bow, wow, wow, wow!"* just like a dog. At the sound of the barking the farmer jumped out of bed, seized his gun, and came to the window, calling out:

"What's the matter?"

"I've caught the thieves!" replied Pinocchio.

"Where?"

"In the hen-house."

"I'll be down at once."

And before you could say "beans" the farmer was there. He walked into the hen-house, caught the Weasels, put them in a sack and said with much satisfaction:

"So I've got you at last! I won't try to punish you, but I'll send you to the next town, where they can make use of your pelts."

Then turning to Pinocchio he said: "How did you happen to discover their plot? My good Rover was never able to catch them!"

The marionette was tempted to tell what he knew about the agreement between the dog and the Weasels. But remembering that the dog was dead, he thought to himself: "What good will it do to accuse the dead? The best thing to do is to let him lie in peace."

"Were you asleep or awake when the Weasels came?" asked the farmer.

"I was asleep," replied Pinocchio, "but they awoke me by whispering together, and one of them came up to me and said, "If you'll promise not to bark and awaken the farmer, we will give you a chicken. How could they have dared to make me such a proposal! I don't propose to help thieves."

"Good boy!" said the farmer patting him on the shoulder. "Such sentiments do you honor. And to show my own gratitude to you, I shall set you free to go on your way."

And he took off the dog-collar.

23 Alone in the World

As soon as Pinocchio felt himself free from that hard and shameful collar, he began to run across the fields, and did not pause a moment until he

122

reached the road which led to the Fairy's house.

When he came to the road he looked ahead. With the naked eye he could see the forest where he had met the Fox and the Cat; and he could even see, above the other trees, the Great Oak to which they had hanged him. But he could not see any trace of the cottage belonging to the Fairy with the Blue Hair.

At this he felt a sad foreboding. He began to run as fast as his legs would carry him, and in a few minutes he reached the field where the white cottage had once stood. But it was no longer there. Instead he saw a marble slab upon the ground, on which any one who could read would have made out these words:

Here Lies

THE FAIRY WITH THE BLUE HAIR

Dead of Grief

Because She Was Forsaken By

HER BROTHER PINOCCHIO

Although Pinocchio could not read, he could spell out the Fairy's name and his own, and he guessed the rest. I leave you to imagine his deep sorrow. He threw himself flat upon the ground, kissed the marble slab a thousand times, and burst into a torrent of weeping. All night long he lay there and wept, and all next morning until he had no tears left. And his cries were so shrill that all the hills round about echoed with them.

"Oh, my Fairy!" he sobbed, "why did you die? Why didn't I die instead of you? I am so naughty and you are so good! And where is my father? Oh, my Fairy, how can I find him? I'll promise never to leave him again—never, never, never! If I could only die too—oh, oh, oh!"

With these and many other cries he worked himself up to such despair that he wanted to tear his hair out by the roots. But being wooden hair he couldn't get hold of it with his fingers.

In the meantime a large Pigeon flying overhead stopped a moment at seeing his distress and called down to him:

"Hello, my boy, what are you doing down there?"

"Can't you see? I'm crying!" said Pinocchio glancing up and drying his eyes with the sleeve of his jacket.

"Tell me," said the Pigeon, "do you know, among your friends, of a marionette by the name of Pinocchio?"

"Pinocchio?—Why I'm Pinocchio!" said the marionette jumping up.

At this reply the Pigeon flew down to the ground. He was as large as a turkey.

"Then you must know a certain Gepetto?" he said to the marionette.

"Do I know him! He is my poor father! Has he sent any word to me? Can you take me to him? Is he still living? Tell me, for pity's sake! Is he still living?"

"I left him three days ago on the seashore."

"What was he doing there?"

"He was making a canoe to cross the ocean. For four months now the poor man has been traveling around in search of you. And not finding you in this country he has decided to go across to foreign lands."

"How far distant is this seashore?" asked Pinocchio anxiously.

"A thousand miles away."

"A thousand miles! Oh, my Pigeon, if I only had wings to fly there!"

"If you want to go, I will carry you."

"How?"

"On my back. Are you heavy?"

"No, indeed! I'm light as a feather."

And without waiting for a second invitation Pinocchio jumped upon the Pigeon's back, and put a leg on each side just like a horseman, calling out contentedly: "Giddap, little horse, I must get there in a hurry!"

The Pigeon rose into the air and soon was touching the clouds. At this great height the marionette had the curiosity to look down; but was at once seized with such fright and dizziness that he clung on for dear life around the bird's neck.

All day long they flew. Toward evening the Pigeon said: "I am very thirsty."

"And I am very hungry," said Pinocchio.

"Then let us stop for a few minutes at this pigeon-house," said his steed; "and later, we can start again. By to-morrow morning early we shall reach the seashore."

They entered the deserted pigeon-house, but found nothing except a pan full of water and a basket of dried peas. In all his life the marionette had never learned to like peas; the very thought of them had turned his stomach. But that night he ate so many of them he was ready to burst; and when he had enough he turned to the Pigeon and said:

"I would never have believed that peas were so good!"

"When there's nothing else to eat the meanest food is delicious," replied the Pigeon. "Hunger has no choice morsels."

Having eaten their hasty meal they resumed their journey. Away they went—all night long —and the next morning they arrived at the sea-coast.

The Pigeon set his passenger down upon the ground, and not caring for thanks or compliments, flew quickly away.

The beach was crowded with people who howled and waved and pointed toward the water.

"What has happened?" asked Pinocchio of an old woman.

"Why, a poor old man who lost his boy has gone out in a canoe to look for him. But the sea is so violent that the little boat is about to be swamped."

"Where is the boat?"

"Over yonder," said the old woman pointing to a tiny speck which at that distance looked no bigger than a nutshell.

Pinocchio gazed at the boat with all his eyes, and presently gave a loud cry:

"It is my father! It is my father!"

As he spoke the little boat, tossed and beaten by the furious waves, went down between the high billows, and then bobbed up again. Pinocchio ran out upon a point of rock and called his father by name, at the same time waving with his hands and cap.

And though Gepetto was so far away from land he recognized his son; for he took off his own cap and waved it in return, as if to say that he would come back if the storm did not prevent.

All at once a terrible wave struck the boat. Those on shore waited for it to come up again, but it was seen no more.

"Poor man!" said the fishers; and mumbling a prayer they turned to leave the strand.

Just then they heard a despairing cry, and turned to see a little boy throw himself from the cliff into the sea, crying, "I will save my father!"

Indeed, Pinocchio being of wood, floated easily and swam like a fish. At times he went under, swept by the current, but again he appeared battling the waves, until he had gone a long distance from the shore. At last he was so far away as to be lost to the sight of those on shore.

"Poor little boy!" said the fishers, and mumbled a prayer for him also.   Then as they could do nothing else they went to their homes.

24 The Isle of Busy Bees

SPURRED on by the hope of finding his father,
Pinocchio swam all night long.   And what a terrible night it was!   It rained, hailed, thundered,

and lightened so that it seemed as bright as day.

But early in the morning he saw a strip of land in the distance. It was an island in the middle of the sea. He redoubled his efforts to reach it, but all in vain. The waves ebbing and flowing formed billows so vast that he was tossed about like a chip. At last by good fortune there came a tremendous wave that lifted him bodily and threw him upon the beach.

He struck the ground with such force that he nearly cracked his bones; but he consoled him· self by saying: "Well, I was lucky to get out alive."

Meanwhile, little by little, the sky cleared; the sun shone in all its splendor; and the sea became as smooth as oil. The marionette spread out his clothes upon the sand, and began to scan the sea far and near in the hope of finding in that immense watery plain some trace of the little boat which carried his father. But all he saw was the sky and the sea, and a ship which looked no bigger than a fly.

"I wonder what's the name of this island?" he said to himself. "I wonder if it has polite people in it, who do not hang boys to trees? But how can I find out if I don't see somebody to ask?"

At this idea of being alone on a deserted island he felt so bad that he began to cry. Just then, however, he saw a large fish swimming along quietly not far away. Not knowing the fish's name he called out in a loud voice:

"Hello, Mr. Fish, will you allow me a word with you?"

"Two of them," replied the Fish who was a Dolphin so polite that you could not find his equal in the sea.

"Will you please tell me if there is a town on this island where one can get something to eat, without running the risk of getting eaten?"

"Certainly," replied the Dolphin; "there's a village not far from here."

"And what road will lead me there?"

"Take the road on the left-hand and follow your nose. You can't miss it."

"Tell me one thing more. You go up and down the sea all the time,—have you chanced to meet a small boat with my father in it?"

"Who is your father?"

"He's the best father in the world, and he has the worst son living."

"His boat must have sunk in the storm."

"And my father——?"

"By this time the terrible Dog-Fish—the terror of all these waters—must have swallowed him."

"Is this Dog-Fish so very big?" asked Pinocchio, beginning to quake with fear.

"Big?—I should say so!" replied the Dolphin. "To give you some idea of it, I will tell you that he is bigger than a five-story house, and has a mouth so large that he can swallow an engine and train of cars at one gulp."

"Good gracious me!" cried the marionette nervously; and turning to the Dolphin he said hurriedly: "I guess I'd better be going. Good-bye, and many thanks for your kindness."

Then he took the road pointed out, and went along it almost at a run. And every time he heard a noise, he looked behind him, for fear he might be followed by that terrible Dog-Fish who was bigger than a five-story house, and whose mouth was so large that it could hold an engine and train of cars.

After hurrying along the road for half an hour he came to a place called "Busy Bee Land." The streets were crowded with people who ran here and there, each busy with his own labors, and all having somthing to do. You couldn't find an idler or a lazy-bones in the whole place.

"Humph!" sniffed Pinocchio, "I'm afraid this is no place for me! I was not born to work."

But meanwhile he was tormented by hunger, as he had not eaten anything for twenty-four hours—not even a dried pea. What was he to do? There were only two ways to get food— either to beg for it or to work for it. He was ashamed to beg, for his father had told him that no one had a right to ask alms except old or in-firm people.

At this moment a man passed along the road, perspiring and out of breath. He was tugging with all his might at two cart-loads of coal. Pin-occhio decided from his looks that he was a kind-hearted man, and went up and said in a low voice:

"Would you be good enough to give a penny to one who is starving?"

"Not one penny," replied the coal-man; "but I'll give you four if you'll help me pull these carts as far as my house."

"What do you take me for?" replied the mari-onette proudly; "I have never played the donkey or pulled a cart in my life."

"The worse for you!" retorted the man. "If

you are really starving, my boy, just eat a couple of slices of your pride, and take care that it doesn't give you indigestion."

The coal-man went on; and after a few minutes another man came by who was a mason, for he carried a basket of lime on his shoulder.

"Kind sir," said Pinocchio, "would you be good enough to give a penny to a poor boy who is starving?"

"Certainly," replied the mason; "come along with me and help carry this lime, and I'll give you five pennies instead of one."

"But the lime is heavy," replied Pinocchio; "and I don't want to tire myself out."

"If you don't want to get tired, my boy, just amuse yourself by yawning for food,—and much good may it do you!"

And he too went on.

In less than half an hour twenty other people came by, and to each of them Pinocchio told his tale of woe; but all answered:

"Shame on you! Instead of looking for work to earn an honest living, you go along the road begging like a vagabond!"

At last a woman came along carrying two pitchers of water.

"Will you please give me a drink of water, good woman?" pleaded Pinocchio who was parched with thirst.

"Certainly, my boy," said the woman setting the pitchers on the ground.

Pinocchio took in water like a sponge; then wiping his mouth he said in a low voice:

"If I could only eat as much as I have drunk!"

On hearing this, the woman said: "If you will carry one of these pitchers home for me I will give you a thick slice of bread."

Pinocchio looked at the pitcher but didn't say "yes" or "no."

"And perhaps I'll give you some meat to eat with the bread," suggested the woman.

Pinocchio looked at the pitcher again, but still didn't say "yes" or "no."

"And perhaps there'll be a sweetmeat to top off with," said the woman.

This was too much to resist, and Pinocchio said: "Why, of course I'll carry the pitcher for you!"

But he found it very heavy; and not being able to manage it with his hands, he placed it on top of his head.

When they reached the cottage the woman

seated Pinocchio at a little table already set, and placed plenty of bread and meat and sugar-plums before him.

Pinocchio did not eat; he stuffed. His stomach seemed a cavern which had been hollow for five months. Then having satisfied his hunger by degrees he lifted his head in order to thank his benefactress. He did not more than look at her, however, when he uttered a long cry of surprise. Then he sat silent with amazement, his eyes bulging out, his fork in air, and his mouth full of food.

"What's the matter?" asked the woman laughing.

"It's you, it's you!" stammered Pinocchio. "Yes, you look like her! yes, and you have eyes like hers—and hair—yes, yes, yes, that's *blue!* Oh, my Fairy, isn't it really you? Don't make me cry any more! Oh, if you only knew how I have suffered, how I have cried! If you only knew!"

And with this outburst, Pinocchio weeping bitterly threw himself on his knees and clasped his arms around the mysterious woman.

25 The Fairy with the Blue Hair Again

At first the good woman pretended that she was not the Fairy with the Blue Hair. But seeing that she was discovered, and not wishing to prolong the comedy, she confessed, saying:

138

"You little rascal! How did you know that it was I?"

"Because I love you so much. That is what told me."

"You remember me, and yet you forgot all I told you. You have been gone so long that now I'm old enough to be your mother."

"And I should like to call you my mother. For such a long time I have wanted a mother just like other boys. But how did you grow up so quickly?"

"That is a secret."

"Then tell it to me, for I want to grow up too."

"But you can't grow," replied the Fairy.

"Why not?"

"Because marionettes never grow. They are born marionettes, they live marionettes, and they die marionettes."

"Oh, I'm so tired of being nothing but a marionette!" cried Pinocchio hitting himself on the head. "I want to grow up to be a *man*."

"Maybe you will become a man if you deserve to be."

"Really? And what do I have to do to deserve it?"

"A very easy thing.   Learn to be a good little boy."

"Am I not a good boy now?"

"Not at all!   Good boys are obedient——"

"And I never mind anybody."

"Good boys like to study and work——"

"And I like to play and run around all the time."

"Good boys always tell the truth——"

"And I don't always."

"Good boys like to go to school——"

"And I have always thought school a dreadful place.   But after this I shall do better."

"You promise me?"

"I promise you.   I want to be a good boy and help my father.—But where is my father now?"

"I cannot say."

"Will I see him again?"

"I think so."

At this reply Pinocchio felt so happy that he seized the Fairy's hands and kissed them.

"Oh, I will be good!" he said.   "And won't you be my mother?"

"Yes, if you will always obey me."

"Willingly, willingly, willingly!"

"Then to-morrow you shall start to school," said the Fairy.

Pinocchio did not seem quite so glad.

"After that you shall choose a trade or profession."

Pinocchio grew very solemn.

"What are you muttering to yourself?" asked the Fairy sharply.

"I was saying—that—that isn't it too late for me to go to school?"

"No sir! It is never too late to learn."

"But I don't care about any trade or profession."

"Why not?"

"Because it makes me tired to work."

"My boy," said the Fairy, "those who talk that way always end in jail or in the poorhouse. Every man, rich or poor, must do something. Woe to the lazy man! Laziness is an evil disease which you must not let seize you in childhood, for when you grow up it cannot be cured."

These words touched Pinocchio's better nature, and raising his head quickly he said to the Fairy: "I will study, I will work, and do what you tell me. I'm tired of being a marionette and want to be a real boy. Didn't you promise that I should be one?"

"Yes, I promised it. Now all depends upon you."

26 Pinocchio Goes to School

THE next day Pinocchio started to school. Just imagine how those mischievous boys behaved when they saw a marionette in their classes!

They laughed out loud. One boy played one trick, another played another. One grabbed his hat out of his hands. Another pulled his coat. Another tried to mark his face with ink. And one even tied strings to his arms and legs to try to make him dance.

For a little while Pinocchio endured this; but at last he lost his patience and said to his tormentors: "Take care! I have not come here to be made sport of. I respect others, and they must respect me."

"Hooray for the clown! He talks like a book!" shouted the little monkeys in great glee; and the rudest of them tried to catch hold of Pinocchio's nose.

But he wasn't quick enough. The marionette suddenly put his foot under the desk and gave him a hard kick on the shins.

"Ouch! what hard feet!" howled the boy, rubbing the bruised place.

"And what elbows! They're like iron," said another, who for his tricks, had got a good blow in the ribs.

Indeed, after a few such blows and kicks, Pinocchio rose in the esteem of the whole school;

and they ended by making a great favorite of him.

The teacher praised him for being so studious. He was the first to reach school in the morning, and the last to leave at night. The only fault to find was that Pinocchio had too many friends, among whom were several who did not like to study. The teacher warned him against these boys, and the good Fairy also advised against them, saying:

"Be careful, Pinocchio. These bad companions will, sooner or later, make you lose your love of books, and may even bring some misfortune upon you."

"No danger of that," boasted the marionette, shrugging his shoulders and tapping his forehead as if to say, "Too much sense here!"

Now it happened, one fine day, while he was going to school he met a group of his friends, who said to him, "Have you heard the great news?"

"No; what news?"

"Why, on the shore near here is a Dog-Fish as big as a mountain."

"Really? I wonder if it's the same Dog-Fish that swallowed my poor father?"

"We are going to the beach to look at him. Don't you want to come along?"

"Not I. I am going to school."

"What good is school, anyway? You can go there to-morrow. One lesson more or less doesn't make any difference."

"But what will the teacher say?"

"Let the teacher spout. That's what he's paid to do."

"But my mother?"

"Your mother won't know anything about it."

"I know what to do," said Pinocchio. "I am very anxious to see the Dog-Fish, but I can wait and go after school."

"Nonsense!" said the boys. "Do you think that a big fish this size is going to wait all day for you? As soon as he gets tired, he'll go away some place else, and then your chance will be gone."

"How long would it take to go there?" asked Pinocchio.

"An hour and a half will take us there and back again."

"Then come on—and the first there is the best man," cried Pinocchio.

At this, away they all went, with their books under their arms! But Pinocchio, always in the lead, seemed to have wings on his feet. From time to time he would look back and make fun of his companions because they could not keep up with him. Seeing them running along panting, blowing and covered with dust he laughed aloud. The unlucky boy did not know what calamity he was running into so gaily.

27 A Free-for-All Fight

As soon as he reached the seashore Pinocchio began to look all around over the water; but he saw nothing of the Dog-Fish. The sea was as smooth as glass.

"Where is the Dog-Fish?" he asked turning to his comrades.

"He has gone for his breakfast," replied one of them laughing.

"Or he may be taking a nap," said another laughing still louder.

From these foolish replies and the laughter, Pinocchio soon saw that he was the victim of a practical joke; and he said angrily:

"Where's the fun? What was the use of telling me that yarn about a Dog-Fish?"

"Because we wanted you to miss a day at school. Aren't you ashamed of being such a goody-good and studying your lessons every day? Aren't you ashamed of yourself?"

"And if I study, what difference does it make to you?"

"It makes a big difference, because you make the rest of us cut a sorry figure with the teacher."

"What do you want me to do, then?"

"You must join us against our three greatest enemies—school, lessons, and teacher."

"But what if I prefer to study?"

"We will have nothing more to do with you, and besides we'll make you pay for it, the first chance we get."

"Pshaw! You make me laugh," said the marionette shaking his head.

"Look out, Pinocchio! Don't you try to bully us!" cried the largest of the boys, shaking his fist. "Don't you come the high-and-mighty over us, either. We don't stand for it! We are not afraid of you. Recollect, we are seven against one."

"Seven dead ones!" mocked Pinocchio.

"Did you hear that? He has insulted us!" cried another.

"Take that back, Pinocchio," shouted a third, "or we'll make you suffer for it!"

"Cuckoo!" jeered Pinocchio.

But just as he said this, the biggest boy hit him on the head. The marionette came back with a blow from his wooden fist which sent the bully staggering; but the other boys closed in and the fight became general.

Pinocchio although alone defended himself like a hero. His feet being of the hardest wood served to keep his foes at a proper distance. Wherever he could land with a strong kick, the boy struck went away howling with a black-and-blue spot.

When the boys found that they couldn't get at him for a hand-to-hand fight, they became angry in earnest and began to look around for something to throw. As there was nothing but sand, they seized their school-books and started to hurl these at the marionette. He was too quick for them, however, and ducked his head so that the books fell into the sea.

Just fancy how surprised the fishes were! They thought the books were something to eat, and at once rose to bite them. But one taste of the front pages and pictures was enough. They made wry faces as much as to say, "None of that stuff for us! We are used to better fare."

Meanwhile the fight grew hotter and hotter, until a large Crab, who had crawled out of the water and was slowly walking up the beach, cried out with a voice like a husky trombone:

"Stop that brawling, you rascals! Stop it at once, I say, or something bad is likely to happen!"

The well-meaning Crab might as well have talked to the wind. Pinocchio turned upon him and said in a surly tone:

"Mind your business, ugly Crab! You'd better eat some seaweed for that husky voice of yours. Go home and go to bed!"

Just then the boys, having thrown all their own books away, happened to see at a little distance the bundle of books belonging to the marionette, and laid hands on them in less time than it takes to tell it. Among these books was a good-sized volume, bound in heavy covers, an Arithmetic. I leave you to guess how heavy it must have been!

One of the little ruffians seized this book and threw it with all his might at Pinocchio. But instead of hitting him it struck one of the other boys on the head. The boy fell to the ground white as a sheet, and could only murmur:

"Oh, my mamma! Help me, for I am killed!"

Then he lay motionless on the sand.

At sight of this dreadful accident, the other boys took to their heels, and in a few minutes were out of sight. But Pinocchio remained. Although scared half out of his wits, he ran to wet his handkerchief in the sea, and with it began to bathe the temples of his poor schoolmate, all the time weeping bitterly, calling him by name, and begging him to open his eyes and speak to him.

While Pinocchio continued to lament and to try to revive his companion, he heard the sound of footsteps. Looking up he saw two policemen approaching.

"What are you doing here?" they asked.

"Trying to help a schoolmate."

"Is he hurt?"

"It seems so."

"I should say so!" said one stooping over the injured boy. "He has been struck in the head. Who did it?"

"Not I," stammered the marionette, hardly able to breathe.

"If you didn't do it, then who did?"

"Not I," repeated Pinocchio.

"And what was it that struck him?"

"It was this book," answered Pinocchio, picking up the heavy Arithmetic.

"Whose book is it?"

"Mine."

"That settles it; nobody else could have done it. Get up at once and come with us."

"But I——"

"Come with us."

"But I am innocent."

"Come with us."

Before starting, the officers hailed some fishermen who were passing not far away in a boat, and said to them, "We will entrust this little wounded boy to your care. Take him home and look after him. To-morrow we will call again."

Then turning to Pinocchio and placing him

between them, they commanded in military tones: "Forward, march! And make haste, or it will be the worse for you!"

The marionette did not wait for a second bidding, but started at once with them along the road which led to the town. But the poor fellow was so confused he didn't know where he was going. It all seemed like a dream—and such an ugly dream! He was nearly crazy. His eyes saw double. His legs trembled. His tongue stuck to the roof of his mouth, and he couldn't utter a single word. And yet in the midst of his stupefaction, a thorn seemed to pierce him to the heart. It was the thought of passing by the good Fairy's house and being seen by her as a culprit guarded by policemen. He would far rather die.

By this time they had reached the edge of the town, and were entering it when a sudden gust of wind blew Pinocchio's hat off and carried it back along the road they had just traversed.

"Will you please let me go after my hat?" asked Pinocchio of his guards.

"Go ahead; but be quick about it."

The marionette ran back and recovered his hat; but instead of putting it on his head, he placed it between his teeth and began to run with all his might toward the sea. He flew as if he were shot out of a gun.

The policemen saw that it would be hard to catch him again, so they set a large Mastiff after him, a dog that had won first prize in all the races. Away went Pinocchio, and the Mastiff close after him. All the people flocked to windows and pavement, eager to see the finish of such an exciting race. But they were disappointed, for the Mastiff and Pinocchio kicked up such a cloud of dust that in a few minutes they were lost to view.

28 In Dire Peril

DURING that desperate race there was one terrible moment when Pinocchio thought himself lost. The Mastiff ran so fast that he all but caught him.

The marionette could feel his hot breath upon his back and could hear his panting. But by good luck the beach was not far away and toward the water he plunged.

With a great leap which saved him from the dog's jaws he sprang into the sea. The Mastiff tried to stop on the edge, but carried forward by his impetus he fell in after him. The unlucky dog did not know how to swim, so he began to thrash about with his feet in order to keep afloat; but the more he kicked the deeper went his head into the water. The first time he came up gasping and strangling, he barked piteously:

"I'm drowning! I'm drowning!"

"Go ahead and drown," replied Pinocchio at a distance, and seeing himself out of danger.

"Help me, dear Pinocchio!" wailed the Mastiff. "Save me from death!"

At this pathetic appeal the marionette, who really had a kind heart, was moved to pity, and turning back to the dog he said, "But if I save you, will you promise not to chase me again?"

"Yes, yes, I promise! But hasten, or I shall go under in another moment!"

Pinocchio hesitated—then remembering that his father had once told him that a good deed is never forgotten, he swam quickly to the drowning dog and seizing him by the tail, soon pulled him out safe and sound upon the beach.

The poor dog could not stand upon his feet. He had swallowed so much salt water that he had swelled up like a balloon. However the marionette did not care to trust himself too much to the Mastiff, so thought it prudent to swim out again.

As he swam away he shouted back: "Goodbye, Mastiff! Luck to you and all your family!"

"Good-bye, Pinocchio!" replied the dog. "A thousand thanks for saving my life. You have done me a great service and one I shall never forget. I hope I shall have the opportunity to repay it some day."

Pinocchio swam on, keeping close to the shore, until at last it seemed a safe place for him to land. He looked at the sand and saw a sort of cave, out of which poured a cloud of smoke.

"There must be fire in that cave," he said to himself; "and so much the better. I will go in and get dry and warm. Then whatever happens, I'm ready for it."

Having formed this plan, he drew near the rocks. But just as he was on the point of landing, he felt something beneath him in the water that rose and rose and rose, and lifted him with it into the air. He tried to escape, but it was too late. To his great astonishment he found himself caught in a huge net swarming with fishes of every form and size, all struggling like himself to get free.

At this moment he saw emerging from the cave a fisherman so ugly that he looked like a sea-monster. Instead of hair he had bunches of green seaweed growing upon his head. Green was the skin of his body; green the color of his eyes; green the hue of his tangled beard which fell below his knees. He looked just like a big lizard walking on its hind legs.

As soon as the fisherman had drawn the net out of the water he said with much satisfaction:

"Ha, a fine catch! To-day I shall have all the fish I can eat."

"Thank goodness, I'm not a fish!" said Pinocchio to himself, taking courage.

The net full of fishes was carried back to the cave, which was gloomy and smoky. In the middle was a great pan full of frying oil which gave out such a rank odor that it almost choked the marionette.

"Now let's see what sort of fish we have!" said

the green fisherman. And thrusting his great flat hand which looked like a spade into the net he pulled out a handful of mullets.

"Fine fellows!" he said, feeling and smelling them eagerly. Then he threw them over into a tub of water.

He did the same thing many times, taking handfuls of fish out of the net, feeling them, and throwing them into the tub. And all the time he was smacking his lips and saying to himself:

"What good whitefish! What exquisite bass! What delicious soles! What choice crabs! What excellent anchovy!"

The last that was left in the net was Pinocchio. When the fisherman picked him up he rolled his green eyes in surprise and fear.

"What sort of a fish is this?" he shouted. "I don't remember eating anything like this before."

He looked him all over, turning him round and round, and then said, "Now I see. It must be a crawfish."

Pinocchio was taken aback when he heard himself called a crawfish, and said sharply, "Crawfish yourself! Be careful how you handle me. You ought to know who I am. I am a marionette."

"A marionette?" said the fisherman. "That's a new kind of fish to me, but so much the better! I shall enjoy eating you all the more."

"Eat me? Don't you understand that I'm not a fish? Don't you see that I talk and think like you do?"

"True enough," rejoined the fisherman; "and since you happen to be a fish that can talk and think like myself, I shall let you decide."

"What do you mean?"

"As a special token of friendship, I shall let you choose which way you want to be cooked. Would you like to be fried in oil, or would you prefer to be stewed in a pan with tomato sauce?"

"To tell you the truth," replied Pinocchio, "if you give me my choice, I would rather be set free, so that I can go back home."

"You are joking! Do you think I would lose the chance to eat a fish as rare as you? Such luck doesn't happen every day, to catch a marionette in these waters. Leave it to me. I shall fry you in the pan with all the other fishes. That ought to suit you. It's some consolation to have plenty of company when you are fried."

At this, the unhappy Pinocchio began to weep and howl.

"Let me go!" he wailed. "Oh, if I had only

gone on to school, and not listened to the other boys! Oh, oh, oh!"

He wriggled and twisted like an eel trying to escape, until the green fisherman took a piece of cord, bound him hand and foot with it, and threw him into the tub with the rest.

Then the man pulled out a box of flour, dipped each of the fish into it, and put them into the pan to fry. One after another they fell into the sizzling oil until at last it came the turn of Pinocchio.

The marionette seeing himself so close to death—and what an awful death!—was seized with such a panic and shook all over so that he didn't have a bit of breath left to beg for mercy. The poor boy looked at his captor piteously. But the green fisherman, paying no heed to him, rolled him all over in the flour, so that he looked like a marionette made of chalk.

Then he took him by the head and—

29 Pinocchio Returns
to the Fairy

JUST as the fisherman was on the point of throwing Pinocchio into the pan, a large dog came into the cave, attracted by the odor of frying fish.

"Get out!" cried the man threateningly, and waving the marionette all covered with flour.

But the dog was as hungry as four ordinary ones, and whined and wagged his tail as much as to say, "Give me a taste of the fish and I will leave you in peace."

"Get out, I say!" repeated the fisherman, and raised his foot to kick him.

Now the dog was not one to be abused, especially when hungry, so he only growled and showed his teeth.

Just then a small hoarse voice was heard crying, "Save me, Mastiff! Save me, or I shall be fried alive!"

The Mastiff—for it was he—at once recognized the voice of Pinocchio, and great was his surprise to find that the voice came from the little floury parcel in the fisher's hand.

Then what did the dog do? Why, he gave one jump from the floor, seized the floury parcel, and holding it gently between his teeth dashed out of the cave like a shot.

The man was in a towering rage at being robbed of the fish which he so much desired to eat, and he ran after the dog. But it was a useless race and he had to be content with the fish that were left.

On ran the Mastiff until he came to the road to the village; then he set his friend gently upon the ground.

"How can I thank you enough?" said the marionette.

"You do not need to thank me," replied the dog; "for you saved me first. I am glad to be able to repay the debt. But if I had reached that cave a minute later——"

"Let's not talk about it!" said Pinocchio shuddering. "Br-r-r-r! It gives me the chills even to think of what a narrow escape I had!"

The Mastiff laughed and stretched out his paw to the marionette, who pressed it warmly in token of friendship. Then they parted company. The dog went home, and Pinocchio went along the road by himself until he reached a hamlet not far away. There he saw an old man seated in an open doorway, and asked him:

"Can you tell me, sir, if you know anything about a little boy, who was wounded by being struck on the head?"

"The boy was carried to this hut by some fishermen, and now——"

"Now he is dead!" interrupted Pinocchio in great grief.

"No, now he has recovered, and has returned to his own home."

"Truly, truly?" cried the marionette dancing with delight. "Then the wound was not serious?"

"No, but it might easily have been, for he was hit upon the head with a heavy book."

"Who threw it?"

"One of his schoolmates—a certain Pinocchio."

"Who is he?"

"They say that he's a bad boy, a vagabond, a good-for-nothing."

"It is not true!" cried the marionette hotly.

"Then you know this Pinocchio?"

"Yes, by sight."

"What do *you* think of him?" asked the old man.

"To me he seems to be a pretty good fellow, fond of studying, obedient, affectionate——"

While the marionette was making up this story he chanced to touch his nose, and found that it was growing longer. Then in a panic he commenced to cry:

"Don't believe a word I'm telling you, good man! I know Pinocchio very well indeed, and

I can assure you that he is a good-for-nothing. He is lazy and disobedient, and instead of going to school, he gets into mischief with bad companions."

As soon as he had said these words, his nose shrank back to its usual size.

"And why are you so white?" the old man now asked.

"I'll tell you. I happened to rub up against a wall which had just been painted," replied the marionette, who was ashamed to admit that he came very near to being fried in a pan, as a fish.

"And your clothes—what has become of them?"

"I fell in with some thieves who stripped me. Please, sir, could you give me some sort of clothes, so that I can go back home?"

"Sorry, my boy, but I haven't a thing except an empty bean bag. If you want that, you're welcome to it."

Pinocchio did not wait to be urged, but took the bag gladly, and after cutting holes in it for his arms, he put it on like a shirt. Lightly dressed in this fashion he started toward the town. But on the way he did not feel easy in his mind. He paused from time to time, saying to himself:

"How shall I ever face the good Fairy? What will she say when she sees me? Will she pardon me a second time? Oh, I'm afraid she won't! And it would serve me right, for I have not kept my promise to her."

By the time he reached the town it was nightfall. A storm came up and it rained very hard, so that he went straight on until he came to the Fairy's house. But once there his courage failed him, and he went by without knocking. He came back to the door a second time, and again did not knock. Then he came back a third time and did not knock. The fourth time he took hold of the knocker tremblingly and let it fall with a light tap.

He waited and waited, and after about half an hour a window on the top floor was thrown open, and Pinocchio saw a large Snail, which carried a light on its head, looking out.

"What do you want at this hour of the night?" said the Snail.

"Is the Fairy at home?" asked the marionette.

"The Fairy is asleep and does not wish to be disturbed. Who are you?"

"Just me!"

"Who is that?"

"Pinocchio."

"Who is Pinocchio?"

"The marionette who lives in this house with the Fairy."

"Ah, I see!" said the Snail; "wait a little and I will come right down."

"Hurry, for pity's sake, for I'm nearly frozen."

"My boy, I'm a Snail, and Snails never hurry."

An hour passed by, then two hours, and the door remained shut. Then Pinocchio being cold and wet knocked again and louder.

At this knock a window lower down was opened and the Snail looked out.

"Beautiful Snail," called Pinocchio, "I have waited two hours and it seems like a year. Please hurry, for pity's sake!"

"My boy," repeated the Snail, "I'm a Snail, and Snails never hurry." And the window was closed.

After a while it struck midnight; then one o'clock; then two o'clock, and still the door remained closed. Pinocchio lost patience and started to take the knocker for a resounding blow, when it turned into a live eel which slipped through his fingers and escaped in a pool of water which lay in the street.

"Ah, so?" cried Pinocchio with growing rage: "if the knocker gets away I shall have to use my foot."

And drawing back a step he gave the panel a furious kick. The blow was so strong that his foot went clear through the wood. The marionette tried to pull it out again, but couldn't succeed. The foot had stuck as fast as if it were riveted in. And there poor Pinocchio had to stay the rest of the night, with one foot on the ground and the other in the air.

In the morning early the door was at last opened. It had taken the good Snail just nine hours to come down the stairs and it was covered with perspiration.

"What are you doing with your foot stuck in the door?" the Snail asked laughing.

"I'm in hard luck. Please see, beautiful Snail, if you can get me out of this fix."

"I'm afraid it will take a carpenter to do that."

"Ask the Fairy to help me."

"The Fairy is asleep and does not wish to be disturbed."

"But would you leave me like this all day?"

"You can amuse yourself by counting the ants that go by."

"At least you might bring me something to eat. I'm starving."

"Directly," said the Snail.

And after about three hours and a half Pinocchio saw it coming back carrying a silver dish. In the dish were a loaf of bread, a leg of chicken and four ripe apricots.

"Here is some breakfast sent you by the Fairy," said the Snail.

At sight of this feast the marionette began to feel better. But imagine his disgust, on beginning to eat, when he found that the bread was plaster, the chicken was cardboard, and the fruit was colored glass! He wanted to cry. He wanted to give up in despair. He wanted to throw everything away. But instead he felt such a gnawing in his stomach that he fainted away.

When he recovered, he found himself lying upon a sofa, and the Fairy standing by him.

"I will forgive you this one time more," she said, "but woe to you if you ever do such things again!"

Pinocchio promised faithfully that he would study and be good. And, in fact, he kept his promise for the rest of the year. He came out first in the school examinations and behaved so

well generally that the Fairy was much pleased
and said to him:

"To-morrow your wish shall be granted at
last."

"And that is——?"

"That you shall cease being a marionette, and
become a real live boy."

You could hardly imagine Pinocchio's joy at
this news so long desired.   All his friends were
to be invited upon the great day for a fine luncheon in the Fairy's house, to celebrate the event.
The Fairy gave orders for two hundred cups of
coffee and four hundred little sandwiches.   The
day promised to be a red-letter one, but—

Unfortunately in the life of a marionette there
is always a *but* to spoil everything!

30 Why There Was No Party

OF course Pinocchio was in a great hurry to go out and invite all his friends to the party. But when he asked the Fairy's permission, she said:

"Yes, you may go, but be sure to return before nightfall. Do you understand?"

"I promise to be back within an hour," answered the marionette.

"Be careful, Pinocchio! Boys are quick to make promises, but are sometimes slow about keeping them."

"But I'm not like other boys. When I say a thing, I mean it."

"We shall see. But if you disobey me, so much the worse for you."

"Oh, I've learned my lesson. I'll be good this time!" laughed Pinocchio as he ran out.

In an hour nearly all of his friends had been invited. Some accepted at once; others hung back a little, until they heard of all the good things to eat, when they ended by saying: "I'll be there sure!"

Now you must know that Pinocchio had one schoolmate whom he liked very much. His real name was Romeo, but the boys had nicknamed him Lampwick because he had a dry, thin, straight little body just like the wick of a lamp. He was the laziest and most mischievous boy in the whole school, but Pinocchio was a great admirer of him. He went quickly to this boy's house to invite him to the luncheon, but didn't find him. He went a second time, and no Lampwick. He went a third time, but all in vain. He sought for him high and low, and at last found him hidden under the porch of a farmer's house.

"What are you doing here?" asked Pinocchio.

"I am waiting until midnight, so that I can go away."

"Where are you going?"

"Oh, a great way off."

"I have been to your house three times to look for you."

"What did you want with me?"

"Haven't you heard of the good luck that has befallen me?"

"What is it?"

"To-morrow I shall cease to be a marionette, and shall become a real boy just like you and the rest."

"May it do you good!"

"To-morrow, therefore, I want you to come to a party at my house."

"But I told you I was going away to-night."

"At what hour?"

"Very shortly."

"Where are you going?"

"I'm going to the most beautiful place in the world—a real paradise!"

"What is its name?"

"It is called 'Playtime Land.' Maybe you'd like to go too?"

"I?—no indeed!"

"That's where you're wrong, Pinocchio! Take my word for it, you'll never regret going. Where could you hope to find a better place for us boys? There are no schools, no teachers, no books. In that blessed land nobody ever studies. There is no school on Saturdays, you know, and every week has six Saturdays and one Sunday in it. Just think of it! Vacation begins the first day of January and ends the last day of December. That's the country for me! That's the way all countries should be!"

"But how does one pass the time in 'Playtime Land?' "

"By playing and having a good time from morning till night. At night you go to bed, and the next morning you do the same thing all over again. How does that strike you?"

"Hum!" said Pinocchio, then nodded his head

slowly as if to say, "It is the sort of life I should like to lead."

"Then will you come with me? Yes or no?"

"No, no, not by any means. I have promised my Fairy to be a good boy, and I wish to keep my word. And now that the sun is setting I must go home at once. So good-bye and a pleasant journey."

"What's your hurry?"

"My good Fairy wants me to be home before night."

"Oh, wait two minutes, can't you?"

"I shall be late."

"Just two minutes."

"And if the Fairy scolds me?"

"Let her scold. When she gets tired she will stop," said the bad boy.

"How are you going—by yourself or with company?"

"By myself? Why, there'll be at least a hundred boys!"

"Are you going on foot?"

"No, a carriage is coming after a while."

"How I should like to see it!"

"Why?"

"Oh, because I want to watch you all start."

"Wait here a little while and you'll see it."

"No, no, I must return home."

"Just another two minutes."

"I've waited too long now. The Fairy will be alarmed about me."

"Poor Fairy! Is she afraid the rats will eat you?"

"But tell me," said Pinocchio, "are you sure that in this country there is no school?"

"Not the shadow of one."

"And no teachers?"

"Not one."

"And you are not obliged to study?"

"Never, never, never!"

"What a delightful country!" said Pinocchio, longingly. "I have never been there, yet I know just how nice it would be!"

"Then why don't you come along?"

"It is useless to tempt me. I have promised the Fairy to be a good boy, and I must keep my word."

"Then good-bye, and give my regards to the other schoolboys."

"Good-bye, Lampwick. A pleasant journey, and remember your friends sometimes."

With this, the marionette took two steps toward home; then he stopped and turning asked: "But are you perfectly sure that there are six Saturdays in the week and only one Sunday?"

"Perfectly sure."

"And do you know for certain that vacation begins the first day of January and ends the last of December?"

"No doubt of it."

"What a beautiful country!" said Pinocchio slowly. Then turning resolutely away he started off in a hurry saying: "Good-bye sure enough, this time."

"Good-bye."

"Oh—how soon do you start?"

"Right away."

"Pshaw! If I were sure you'd start in an hour, I'd wait."

"And the Fairy?"

"Well, I'm late now anyway; and an hour more or less will not matter."

"Poor Pinocchio! What if she should scold?"

"Let her scold. When she gets tired she will stop."

Meanwhile it became quite dark; and after a while they saw a little light moving far off down the road. It drew nearer and they heard the jingling of bells and the blowing of tiny trumpets so far away they sounded like mosquitoes.

"There they come!" exclaimed Lampwick, jumping up.

"Who?" asked Pinocchio in a low voice.

"It's the carriage with the others. Now are you going? Yes or no?"

"But is it really true that boys are not obliged to study there?"

"Never, never, never!"

"What a delightful country! What a beautiful country!"

31 In Playtime Land

AT last the carriage arrived; and it drew up without making the least noise, for the wheels were wrapped with rags. It was drawn by twelve pairs of donkeys, all of the same size, but of different colors. Some were gray, some were brown, and some were dappled. But the strangest thing about them was the fact that instead of having shoes made out of iron, like other beasts of burden, they wore leather shoes shaped just like yours or mine.

And the driver? Picture for yourselves a short, fat, round man shaped like a butterball, with an oily smile, a little mouth that was always laughing, and a coaxing sort of voice just like that of a cat when he is asking for something to eat. Every boy who saw him liked him at once, and lost no time in scrambling into his carriage. They wanted him to take them to that paradise marked on the geographies under the name of "Playtime Land."

And so, on this occasion, the carriage was filled with boys eight to twelve years old, packed like sardines in a box. They were huddled in so tight that they could scarcely breathe, but no one said "Ouch," or made any complaint. The thought that in a few hours they would find themselves in a country where there were no books, nor schools, nor teachers, made them so happy that they could afford to overlook the present hardships, such as hunger, thirst, or lack of sleep.

As soon as the carriage stopped, the driver turned to Lampwick, smiled upon him, and said in a fawning voice:

"Tell me, my fine lad, do you wish to go with us to that happy land?"

"Indeed I do, sir!"

"But I must warn you, my child, that the carriage is full—entirely full, as you can see."

"That's all right," replied Lampwick. "I'd just as soon sit up on the box with you."

And with a leap he mounted up to a place beside the driver.

"And you, my dear," said the driver beaming down blandly upon Pinocchio; "what will you do? Will you come along, or remain behind?"

"Oh, I stay behind," replied Pinocchio. "I must go back home, and go to school, as all good boys do."

"Much good may it do you!"

"Listen to me, Pinocchio," said Lampwick. "Better come with us and we will have a fine time."

"No, no, no."

"Come with us and we will have a fine time," shouted all the other boys.

"But if I go with you, what will the good Fairy say?" said the marionette who began to feel as if he were pulled along by the sleeve.

"Do not get such gloomy notions into your head. Think of the happy land we are going to, where we shall be our own masters and play around all day long."

Pinocchio's only answer at first was a sigh—then another sigh—then a third sigh. Finally he said: "Find a seat for me and I will come."

"All the seats are full," replied the driver, "but I will gladly give up my seat on the box to you."

"And you?"

"I will walk."

"No, indeed, I can't allow that!" said Pinocchio. "I would like to ride upon the back of one of those donkeys."

With this, he went up to one of the leaders and tried to mount it; when the little beast gave him a sudden kick which landed him upon the ground. Of course the other boys burst out with rude and jeering laughter at this. But the driver did not laugh. He came softly up to the donkey and pretended to pet it, but really pinched its ear savagely.

Meanwhile Pinocchio, very angry at finding himself upon the ground, gave another jump for the animal's back, and he jumped so well that the boys quit laughing and began to shout "Hurrah for Pinocchio!" at the same time clapping their hands.

But just as they were ready to start, the donkey shot out its hind feet so suddenly that the marionette was hurled to the middle of the road and landed on a heap of gravel. Then the boys roared again. But the driver, instead of laughing, went softly up to the donkey and pretended to say something to it, while on the sly he pinched its other ear very cruelly. Then he said to the marionette:

"Now get on and don't be afraid. The donkey had some notion in his head, but I have told him it is all right."

So Pinocchio mounted again, and this time they started on. But while the donkeys galloped ahead, the marionette fancied that he heard a low, scarcely audible voice say to him:

"Poor dunce! You want to do as you please, but you will be sorry for it!"

Pinocchio, somewhat scared, looked on every side to see whence came these warning words, but he could see no one. The donkeys galloped on, the carriage rolled, the boys had become quiet, Lampwick was nodding, and the driver hummed contentedly to himself.

They went another mile, and again Pinocchio heard the whispered voice, which said:

"Simpleton, bear this in mind! The boys who give up study, throw away their books, won't listen to their teachers, and do nothing but amuse themselves, always come to some bad end. I know what I am talking about! I've been through it all. The day will come when you'll cry your eyes out, but that will be too late!"

At these faint words, the marionette was more alarmed than ever. He jumped off the donkey's back and started to pat it upon the nose. Imagine his surprise when he found the little steed in tears; and he was crying just like a boy!

"I say, Mr. Driver!" called Pinocchio; "do you know something strange? This donkey is crying!"

"Let him cry. He will laugh when he gets some hay."

"But who taught him how to talk?"

"He learned a few words from having been three years with a troupe of trained dogs."

"Poor beast!"

"Come, come!" said the driver. "We must not waste our time upon a donkey who is crying. Remount your steed and let us go. The night is cool and the journey is long."

Pinocchio did so. The carriage ran on, and by morning had reached the country with the delightful name of "Playtime Land."

This country was like no other place in the world. The whole population was made up of boys. The oldest were only fourteen years old, the youngest were over eight. In the streets was a continual racket, a hooting and yelling that would drive you crazy. There were bands of urchins everywhere. Some played marbles or ball; others rode velocipedes or wooden horses. Some played hide-and-seek; others tag. Some went around dressed like clowns and tooting horns. Some sang, or made speeches, or walked on their hands, or laughed, or whistled. Others cackled like a hen that has just laid an egg. In a word, it was a regular pandemonium—such an uproar that you would want to stuff cotton in your ears.

The moment that Pinocchio, Lampwick and all the other newcomers set foot in the city, they at once mingled with the motley throng, and in a few minutes had become friends with everybody. Who could be happier than they? It was glorious!

And thus, amid a continual good time and merrymaking, the hours, the days and the weeks sped by like lightning.

"Oh, what a beautiful life!" exclaimed Pinocchio every time he happened to meet Lampwick.

"See—was I not right?" replied the other. "And to think that you didn't want to come! You actually wanted to return to that Fairy of yours and waste your time studying! If to-day you are freed from all books and school, you owe it to me, to my advice and urging. Only true friends can do such favors as this."

"It is true, Lampwick. I have you to thank for it all. And yet my teacher was always saying: 'Do not have anything to do with that rascal, Lampwick; he is a bad boy and will give you bad advice.'"

"Poor teacher!" replied the other wagging his

head. "I'm afraid I really did give him a good deal of trouble. But I forgive him!"

"Noble soul!" said Pinocchio embracing him.

In this fashion five months slipped away. They spent the whole day in idleness and games, without once opening a book or seeing a school.

Then came a morning when Pinocchio awoke to a very disagreeable surprise, which indeed put him in an unhappy frame of mind.

32 The Donkey Fever

WHAT then had happened?

I will tell you, my dear little reader. The surprise which awaited Pinocchio on waking was this. He reached up to scratch his head, and found—now what do you suppose he found? He found to his tremendous amazement that he had *ears* longer than his hand, growing on each side of his head!

You will remember that when he was born he had such tiny ears nobody could see them. So just imagine his surprise now to find them grown so long during the night. He ran to look at himself in a glass; but finding none, he poured some water into a basin, and looking into it he saw something he did not like to see—his own face set off by a pair of fine donkey's ears!

I leave you to picture the grief, shame and despair of poor Pinocchio. He began to cry and howl and beat his head against the wall. But his ears continued to grow and grow and to sprout hair along the edges.

On hearing his loud screams, a Mouse who lived on the lower floor entered the room; and seeing the marionette's distress he asked kindly:

"What is the matter, neighbor?"

"I'm sick, friend Mouse, very sick indeed, and it is a kind of malady which frightens me. Do you know anything about feeling a pulse?"

"A little."

"Feel mine, then, and see if I have a fever."

The Mouse felt Pinocchio's pulse with one of his forepaws, and then said:

"My friend, it grieves me to have to give you bad news."

"What is it?"

"You have an ugly fever."

"What kind?"

"The donkey fever."

"I don't know what kind that is," replied the marionette, who knew only too well.

"Then I will explain it. You must know that in two or three hours you will no longer be a marionette, nor a boy. You will turn into a donkey just like those others that pulled the carriage when you came here."

"Oh, poor me! poor me!" wailed Pinocchio, pulling at his ears with both hands, as if he would tear them out by the roots.

"My friend," said the Mouse consolingly, "what are you doing? You ought to know it is a wise decree, that all lazy boys who dislike books, schools and teachers, and who do nothing but play all day long, must end sooner or later by turning into donkeys."

"Is that really true?" asked the marionette sobbing.

"Too true! Now it is too late to cry about it. You should have thought of this before."

"But it wasn't my fault! Believe me, dear Mouse, it was all the fault of Lampwick."

"Who is he?"

"A schoolmate of mine. I wanted to go back home, and be obedient, and study hard; but Lampwick said: 'What's the use? Come along with me to Playtime Land, and you won't have to study at all; for there we shall have a good time and play around from morning till night.'"

"And why did you follow the advice of your false friend?"

"Why? Why, because, my friend Mouse, I haven't a grain of sense! Oh, if I had only stayed with the Fairy who loved me and did so much for me! By this time I should be a real boy. Oh, just wait till I get at that Lampwick!"

And he started toward the door. But when he got there he remembered about his donkey's ears, and not wishing to display them in public he thought of a plan. He made a tall cotton cap and pulled it down on his head, well over his ears.

Then he went out and began to look for Lampwick. He looked in the streets, in the square, in

the theatre, everywhere, but couldn't find him.
He asked several people he met, but no one had
seen him.   Then he went to his house and
knocked upon the door.

"Who's there?" called out Lampwick.

"It is I," replied the marionette.

"Wait a moment and I'll let you in."

After about half an hour the door was opened;
and Pinocchio was surprised to see that his friend
also wore a huge cotton cap, which was pulled
clear down to the tip of his nose.   At sight of this
cap, Pinocchio felt somewhat consoled, for he
thought to himself: "Perhaps he has the same
sort of complaint I have."

But he pretended not to see anything, and
asked smiling: "How are you to-day, my dear
Lampwick?"

"Fine!—Like a mouse in a cheese-cake."

"Do you mean it?"

"Why shouldn't I?"

"Excuse me; but why have you got that big
cap pulled over your ears?"

"My doctor ordered me to wear it on account
of having stiff knees.   But you, dear Pinocchio,
why are *you* wearing one?"

"My doctor prescribed it because I stubbed my toe."

"Oh, poor Pinocchio!"

"Oh, poor Lampwick!"

Then they were both silent for a long while, and stood gazing at each other. At last the marionette said coaxingly to his friend:

"Relieve my curiosity, dear Lampwick. Have you ever suffered with your ears?"

"Never! And you?"

"Never! But since morning, I have felt some little trouble."

"So have I."

"Really? In which ear?"

"Both of them. And you?"

"Both of them. Can it be the same disease?"

"I fear so."

"Will you do me a favor, Lampwick?"

"Certainly."

"Show me your ears."

"No, indeed! But show me yours first, Pinocchio."

"No, indeed! But I'll tell you what let's do. Let's take off our caps at the same time."

"All right. One, two, three!"

And at the "three," both took off their caps and threw them away.

And then something took place which would seem beyond belief if it weren't true. As soon as Pinocchio and Lampwick saw that they had been smitten by the same disease, instead of feeling humiliated, they began to poke fun at the other's enormous ears, until they finally burst out laughing. They laughed and laughed and laughed until they could hardly stand up.

All at once Lampwick ceased his laughter, became deadly pale, and called to his friend:

"Save me, save me, Pinocchio!"

"What's the matter?"

"Oh, my! I can't stand up!"

"I can't either!" cried Pinocchio weeping and trembling.

And as they spoke they fell down upon all fours and began to run around the room. At the same time their arms turned into forelegs, their faces grew long, and their bodies were covered with stiff grizzled hair. But the most horrible moment for each came when they felt a long tail swishing along behind them!

Overcome by grief and shame they tried to bemoan their fate. But instead of human cries,

they began to bray like donkeys, "Hee-haw!
Hee-haw!"

At this moment there came a knock at the
door, and a voice was heard calling:

"Open the door! I am your driver,—the one
who drove the carriage that brought you here.
Open at once, I say, or it will be the worse for
you!"

33 A Donkey's Fate

SEEING that the door did not open, the driver
commenced to kick it violently until it burst
open. Then he entered the room and said to
Pinocchio and Lampwick, with his usual oily
smile:

"Good boys! You bray first rate. I recognized your voices at once, and so have come to take you away."

At these words the two little donkeys hung their heads and stood silent, with ears drooping and tails between their legs.

At first the driver patted them and soothed them; then taking out a curry-comb he gave them a good currying. When he had done this so vigorously that they shone like two mirrors, he put a bridle on each of them and led them to the market-place, with a view to selling them at a good price. And, in fact, buyers were not long in coming.

Lampwick was bought by a farmer whose donkey had died the day before from overwork; while Pinocchio was sold to the manager of a company of clowns and ring performers, so that he could be trained to jump and dance with the other trick animals.

And now, my little readers, do you know what trade that driver followed? That smooth-faced villain went everywhere with his carriage; and whenever he found any lazy boys who hated books and schools, he cajoled them to come with him. And when he had filled his carriage he would take them to Playtime Land, where they spent all their time in idle fun. After these poor deluded boys had spent a certain length of time in this manner, they always turned into donkeys —just like Pinocchio and Lampwick—and then the driver took them and sold them. In this way he became a rich man.

What happened later to Lampwick I do not know. As for Pinocchio, he led a hard, weary life of it. When he was led to his new quarters, his master filled the manger with chopped straw; but Pinocchio, after taking a mouthful of it, spat it out again. Then the master, growling, put down some hay; but that didn't suit, either.

"Oh! you do not even like hay?" cried the master enraged. "All right, my fine fellow, if you have such notions as this in your head, we'll see if we can't get them out!"

And taking a whip he gave Pinocchio a sound cut across the legs. In great pain Pinocchio brayed aloud, and this is what he said:

"Hee-haw! hee-haw! I don't like straw!"

"Then try hay," replied his master, who understood donkey talk very well.

"Hee-haw! hee-haw! Hay gives me the stomach-ache."

"So you think, then, that a donkey ought to be fed on chicken and capon and jelly?" sneered the man, and gave him another cut with the whip.

At this second blow, Pinocchio thought it wise to keep his mouth shut, so said no more. The man closed the stable door and went away. Pinocchio was alone, and as he had eaten nothing for several hours, he began to yawn from hunger. When he yawned he opened his mouth so wide it looked like an oven.

He began to hunt around, but finding no other food he resigned himself to nibbling a little of the hay; and having chewed a good mouthful, he shut his eyes and swallowed it.

"This hay isn't so bad after all," he said to himself, and fell to eating it with a relish.

The next morning on awakening he began to hunt for some more hay, but couldn't find any, as he had eaten it all during the night. So he took a mouthful of the chopped straw and tried that. He could not persuade himself it was as good as rice with cream, or macaroni with cheese; but he managed to eat it, saying to himself, "Hard luck!"

"Hard luck, nonsense!" called the master, who just then entered the stall. "Do you think, my high and mighty, that I bought you just to watch you eat and drink? Not by a jugful! I bought you to put you to work, so that you can earn a lot of money for me. So, out with you, my hearty! Come with me to the sawdust ring, and I will teach you to jump through a hoop and to bow. After that you must learn to dance upon your hind-legs."

Poor Pinocchio had to do as the man said, and learn a lot of tricks. It took him three months, and he got many a blow for his pains.

But at last came the day when his master was ready to announce a truly wonderful show. Posters of many colors were put up on every street, to tell what Pinocchio could do.

That night, as you may easily guess, an hour before the time for the show to begin, the theatre was crowded. The whole house swarmed with children of all ages, down to tiny tots, eager to see the dancing of the famous donkey, Pinocchio.

After the end of the first part of the performance, the manager, dressed in a long black coat, close-fitting white trousers, and leather riding boots which reached to his knees, came before the audience, made a low bow and began a grandil-

GRAND GALA PERFORMANCE!

WILL TAKE PLACE TO-NIGHT

Wonderful Jumps!

Surprising Feats!

By All the Artists of the Company

And by All the Horses

 **SPECIAL**

There will be presented for the first time

THE FAMOUS DONKEY

Pinocchio

RIGHTLY CALLED

THE DANCING STAR!

THE THEATRE WILL BE AS BRIGHT AS DAY.

oquent speech sounding the praises of his wonderful donkey.

"This celebrated artist has already had the honor of dancing before all the crowned heads of Europe," he ended.

His speech was greeted with much laughter and applause, which was redoubled until it became like a hurricane when they saw Pinocchio come into the middle of the ring. He was dressed very gaily. He had a new bridle of shining leather with buckles of polished brass. Two white tassels hung from his ears. His mane was woven into many plaits, each tied with red silk. A broad band of gold and silver went round his body; and his tail was interwoven with many-colored ribbons. In a word, he was the finest donkey ever!

The manager presented him to the audience with another flowery speech, telling how he had found a savage animal roving at large in the torrid zone; how all his efforts to tame him had been of no avail; and how at last he had discovered a small bone in the animal's head, which showed a fondness for dancing. So he had devoted his efforts in that direction, with the happy result that here before them they had Pinocchio, the Dancing Star!

Then the manager made another low bow, and turning to the donkey, said:

"Now, Pinocchio! Before beginning your tricks, pray salute this fine audience of gentlemen, and ladies, and children!"

Pinocchio obediently knelt down upon the knees of his fore-legs, and remained kneeling until the manager, cracking his whip, cried out:

"Now march!"

The donkey then stood up again and began to go around the ring, but always keeping step.

"Now trot!" commanded the master. And Pinocchio began to trot.

"Now gallop!" And Pinocchio began to gallop.

"Now full speed!" And Pinocchio began to run as fast as he could.

But while he was going like a Barbary horse, the manager raised his arm and fired a pistol. At this, the donkey, pretending to be wounded, fell sprawling in the ring and lay stiff as though really dead.

Rising from the ground amid a burst of applause which seemed to lift the roof, Pinocchio chanced to look upward—and there he saw a beautiful lady in the balcony, who had on a golden necklace, from which hung a locket; and this locket contained the picture of a marionette!

"That is my picture!   That lady is my Fairy!" cried Pinocchio to himself, recognizing her at once.   And overcome with joy he tried to cry out, "Oh, my Fairy!   Oh, my Fairy!"

But instead of these words there came from his throat such a prolonged braying that it made all the spectators laugh, especially all the boys.

Then the manager, in order to teach him better manners than to bray in public, gave him a cut of the whip on the end of his nose.   The poor little donkey thrust out his tongue and licked his nose about five minutes, it hurt him so.   But what was his despair, on looking upward a second time, when he saw that the balcony seat was empty and the Fairy had disappeared.   He felt as if he should die.   His eyes filled with tears and he began to weep bitterly.   No one seemed to notice it, not even the manager, who cracked his whip, crying:

"Try again, my good Pinocchio!   Now show

these ladies and gentlemen with what grace you can jump through these hoops."

Pinocchio tried two or three times; but every time he came to a hoop, instead of jumping through it he ran underneath it. At last he jumped through; but his hind-leg got caught in the hoop and he stumbled and fell to the ground. When he tried to get up he was lame, and they could hardly lead him to his stall.

"Bring out Pinocchio! We want the donkey! Bring out the donkey!" shouted all the boys in the pit, who felt sorry that he was hurt.

But the donkey could not appear any more that night.

The next morning the veterinary—that is the doctor of animals—looked him over, and then said that he was lamed for life. So the manager said to the stable-boy:

"What use have we for a lame donkey? He would only be another mouth to feed. Take him to the market-place and sell him."

The boy led him away limping, and when they reached the square they soon found a buyer who wanted to know the price.

"Four dollars," answered the boy.

"I will give you twenty-five cents for him. Do not think that I can make any use of him; I want only his skin. I see that it is very tough and I can make a good drum-head out of it."

Just imagine how delighted Pinocchio must have felt, when he heard that he was to be skinned for a drum-head!

The boy took the quarter, as that was the best price he could get, and the buyer led the donkey up on top of a cliff bordering the seacoast; and having tied a stone to his neck, and fastened a rope to him, he held the other end of the rope and pushed the beast over the edge into the water.

Pinocchio sank at once to the bottom, because of the stone. The man, holding one end of the rope, sat down and waited until the donkey should have time to drown. Then he proposed to pull him up and skin him.

34 The Terrible Dog-Fish

AFTER the donkey had been under water for about five minutes, the man who was holding the rope said to himself:

"By this time the lame beast must be drowned.

So let's hoist him up and make a fine drum out of his hide."

And he began to pull up the rope. He pulled and he pulled and he pulled, until at last he saw coming to the surface—what do you suppose? Instead of a dead donkey, he saw a marionette very much alive and wriggling on the rope like an eel!

At sight of a wooden marionette the man thought that he must be dreaming. His mouth opened, and his eyes stuck out of his head from amazement. When he had recovered a little from his first shock, he asked stammering:

"What has become of that donkey I threw in the sea?"

"I'm the donkey," replied the marionette smiling.

"You!"

"Yes, I."

"Rascal, don't make fun of me!"

"But I'm not, my dear fellow. I am in dead earnest."

"Then how does it happen that you've turned into a marionette?"

"Perhaps it's the effect of the salt water. The sea does queer things."

"Be careful, marionette, be careful! Do not think you can have fun at my expense. It will be the worse for you, if I lose my temper!"

"Well, then, do you want to know the truth? Untie me, and I'll tell you."

Curious to know the true story of this strange event, the buyer untied the rope which bound the marionette, and Pinocchio once more felt himself free as a bird. Then to keep his promise, he sat down and told the astonished man all that had lately happened to him, up to the time he became a lame donkey.

"Then you bought me, you know," he added.

"That's true," nodded the man dolefully. "And to think I paid a quarter of a dollar for you! Now who will give me my money back?"

"Why did you buy me? Just to make a drum-head out of me. A drum-head!"

"I admit it—but where am I to find another skin?"

"Do not despair. There are plenty of donkeys left in the world!"

"Humph! Is that all there is to your story?"

"No, there are a few words left," answered Pinocchio. "After you bought me, you led me to this cliff to kill me, but being a very merciful man you decided to throw me over and let me drown. Much obliged for your kindness, I am sure! For the rest, you would probably have succeeded in your plan, if it hadn't been for the Fairy."

"What Fairy is that?"

"My good Fairy with the Blue Hair, who has been like a mother to me. As soon as she saw that I was in danger of being drowned, she sent a great school of fishes who began to eat my donkey body. What mouthfuls they took! I shouldn't have thought that fishes were greedier than boys! When they had eaten all the flesh, they came to the bones, or rather to the wood. You must know that I am made out of very hard wood, and after the first bite, they found I was bad for their teeth; so they swam away disgusted, without so much as saying, 'Thank you!' Pretty soon you pulled me up, and here I am."

"And do you expect me to believe such a yarn?" cried the man in a rage. "All I know is that I spent twenty-five cents for you, and I want my money back. Do you know what I shall do? I shall carry you back to the market-place and sell you for kindling-wood."

"All right; that suits me!" said Pinocchio.

And as he spoke he jumped off the cliff into the sea, where swimming easily out from the shore he called back, "Good-bye! If you ever want another drum-head, don't forget me!"

Then he laughed and swam a little farther, and turned around and shouted still louder, "Good-bye! If you ever want some good kindling-wood, don't forget me!"

By this time he was so far away as to be only a little black spot on the surface of the water. Now and again he would throw his whole body out and jump and tumble like a playful dolphin. While he thus swam, he chanced to see far off a rock which looked like white marble; and on the top of this rock stood a pretty little Goat, bleating at him in a friendly way and making signs for him to come near.

The most singular thing about this Goat was the fact that, instead of having a white, black, or mottled coat like other goats, it had *blue hair*— just like that of the beautiful Fairy!

I leave you to imagine how strongly Pinocchio's heart beat as he drew near and saw this for himself. Redoubling his efforts he swam toward the rock, and, indeed, was half-way there when he saw coming toward him out of the water the horrible head of a sea-monster. Its mouth was open like an immense cavern, and it had three rows of tusks which would frighten you merely to see a picture of them.

It was the terrible Dog-Fish!

At sight of this most dreaded monster of the sea, poor Pinocchio was almost dead from fright. He tried to dodge it and to swim away, but could make no headway against that immense open mouth which always pointed toward him, and came on with the speed of a hurricane.

"Make haste, Pinocchio, for pity's sake!" bleated the pretty little Goat.

Pinocchio splashed desperately with arms and chest and legs and feet.

"Oh, hurry, Pinocchio! He's gaining on you!"

Pinocchio swam with all his might.

"Quick, quick!" called the Goat. "If you waste a moment, you are lost! Hurry, hurry!"

On came Pinocchio, and the monster right after him, racing together like musket-balls. As they neared the rock, the Goat came to the very edge and held out her two front feet to help him out of the water.

But it was too late! The monster was upon

him, and drawing in its breath swallowed him as easily as if he had been an egg. So violently did he go down, that he fell into the stomach of the Dog-Fish with great force and lay stunned for a quarter of an hour.

When he had recovered his senses a little he did not know where he was. It was very dark all around him—so dark that he felt as if he had stuck his head into an ink-bottle. He listened intently, but could hear no sound. Once in a while he seemed to feel a gust of wind striking his face. At first he did not know where it came from, but afterward decided it must be from the monster's lungs.

At first Pinocchio tried to pluck up a little courage; but when he became certain that he was shut up in the stomach of the sea-monster, he lost all hope and began to cry and scream for help at the top of his voice.

"Who's there?" called a hoarse voice some distance off.

"Who are you?" replied Pinocchio nearly frozen with fear.

"I am a poor Tunny-fish who was swallowed at the same time you were. What sort of a fish are you?"

"I am not a fish at all.   I'm a marionette."

"Then if you aren't a fish, how did you come to be swallowed?"

"I don't know.   I didn't want to be!   Now what are we going to do, down here in the dark?"

"We must resign ourselves to fate and wait until the monster has digested us."

"But I don't want to be digested!" howled Pinocchio.

"Neither do I.   But I'd rather die this way than to be soaked in vinegar and oil like a sardine."

"Nonsense!" said Pinocchio.

"That is my opinion at any rate," replied the Tunny, "and should be respected as such."

"Very well—but I wish to get out of this—to escape, some way."

"Escape if you can."

"Is this Dog-Fish very long?"

"About a mile, I guess, without counting the tail."

While they were thus talking, Pinocchio thought he could see in the distance a flicker of light.

"I wonder what that light could be?" he said.

"Probably some companion in distress, who is also waiting to be digested."

"I believe I will find out. It might be some old fish who could show us a way of escape."

"Well, I wish you good luck."

"Good-bye, Tunny."

"When shall we meet again?"

"Who knows? It's better not to think about it!"

35 Gepetto
in Strange Quarters

As soon as he had bidden the friendly Tunny
good-bye, Pinocchio began to grope forward in
the darkness. Trying to walk upright in the Dog-

Fish's body, he went on a step at a time in the direction of the little light which shone so far away. As he walked, he felt his feet splashing in a stream of greasy, slippery water which gave forth the odor of fried fish so strongly that he thought the monster must be keeping Lent.

The further he went, the brighter grew the light. At last, step by step he reached it—and what do you suppose he found? You couldn't guess in a thousand times. He found a table ready set, and lighted by a candle stuck in a green glass bottle. And seated at the table was a little old man with a white beard, who was trying to make a meal out of some frisky minnows.

On seeing this old man, Pinocchio was almost overcome with joy. He wanted to laugh; he wanted to cry; he wanted to call on him, all at once. But instead he made a confused choked-up sound in his throat. At last came a great cry of joy, and rushing to the old man he threw his arms around his neck sobbing out:

"Oh, father, father! Have I found you at last? I shall never leave you again—never, never, never!"

"Do my eyes tell me the truth?" exclaimed the old man; "or is it really my dear Pinocchio?"

"It is! It is no one else! And you have already forgiven me, really, haven't you? Oh, father, how good you are! And to think that I have been so bad! If you only knew the scrapes I have got into, since that day when you sold your coat to buy me a spelling-book!"

Then Pinocchio told him very truthfully about all his adventures, which my little readers already know. And Gepetto, in his turn, told how his boat had been capsized that stormy day at sea.

"Then this terrible Dog-Fish came along and stuck out his tongue and swallowed me as easily as if I had been a bologna sausage," Gepetto ended.

"How long have you been shut up in here?" asked Pinocchio.

"Almost two years. Two years, my Pinocchio, but they seem like two centuries!"

"But how have you managed to live? Where did you get your candles? And your matches?"

"I'll tell you all about it. You must know that the same storm which wrecked my boat also swamped a trading ship. The sailors all saved themselves, but the ship sank to the bottom, where this greedy Dog-Fish swallowed the whole thing."

"What! You don't mean to say that he swallowed it at one mouthful!" said Pinocchio in astonishment.

"Yes, at one mouthful. Only he did not fancy the mainmast which got wedged between his teeth like a toothpick. Fortunately for me, the ship was loaded not only with preserved meat in tin boxes, but also with biscuit, toasted bread, bottles of wine, dried grapes, cheese, coffee, sugar, candles, and matches. With all this godsend I have managed to live for two years, but to-day I am at the end of my resources. There is nothing left of my store of food, and this candle which you see is the last of the stock."

"And after it is gone—?"

"We shall be in the dark, my boy."

"Then there's no time to lose, father," said Pinocchio. "We must flee at once."

"Flee? Where?"

"We must make our escape from the mouth of the Dog-Fish, and throw ourselves in the sea."

"You have a good idea, my dear Pinocchio, but I do not know how to swim."

"What difference does that make? You can get on my back, for I am a good swimmer, and I will carry you safe and sound to shore."

"You are dreaming, my boy!" replied Gepetto shaking his head sadly. "Do you think it possible for a marionette half as big as I am to swim and carry me on his shoulders?"

"Try me and see! In any event, if it is fated that we must die, we shall have the consolation of dying together."

And without further parley, Pinocchio picked up the candle and started on in advance saying, "Follow me and don't be afraid."

They managed to go a good distance, traversing the entire length of the Dog-Fish's stomach. But when they came to the place where the great throat began, they stopped and began to think over the best plan for getting out.

Now, you must know that the Dog-Fish, being very old, was afflicted with poor lungs and a weak heart, so he had to sleep with his mouth open. For this reason, Pinocchio looking up through the long gullet could see right out of the enormous mouth and catch a glimpse of the starry sky and beautiful moonlight.

"Now is our time!" he whispered to his father. "The Dog-Fish is sleeping like a dormouse, the sea is calm, and it is as bright as day. After me, father. and we shall soon be safe."

So at once they climbed up the gullet of the monster, reached the base of the immense mouth, and began to tiptoe softly over the tongue—a tongue so wide and long that it seemed like the court of a garden. But just as they were about to give a great leap into the sea, the Dog-Fish sneezed so violently that they were hurled backward and fell clear to the bottom of his stomach. So swiftly had they come that their candle was blown out and they were left in utter darkness.

"What next?" asked Pinocchio, growing serious.

"This time we are indeed lost," his father replied in despair.

"Not yet! Take my hand, father, and be careful not to slip."

"Where will you lead me?"

"We must try again. Come with me and have no fear."

Again they set out, Pinocchio leading Gepetto, and climbed laboredly up the stomach and through the windpipe. Then they went the length of the tongue and climbed over the three rows of cruel teeth. Before making the great leap into the sea, the marionette said to his father:

"Now get upon my back, clasp your arms

tightly round my neck, and leave the rest to me."

Gepetto did so, and the brave Pinocchio threw himself boldly into the water and began to swim. The sea was as smooth as oil. The moon shone in all her glory; and the Dog-Fish slumbered so soundly that not even a cannon would have awakened him.

36 Some
Old Acquaintances

WHILE Pinocchio swam as fast as he could to
reach the shore, he noticed that his father, who
sat astride his shoulders with his feet in the water,

was trembling as though he had the fever. Was
he quaking from cold or from fright? Who could
say? Perhaps it was partly from both. But Pinocchio, thinking that he was afraid, tried to re-
assure him.

"Courage, father," he said. "In a few minutes
we shall be safe on shore."

"But where is that blessed land?" asked the
old man, becoming still more alarmed and searching with his eyes far and near. "I can see nothing in any direction except sea and sky."

"But I can see a beach," said the marionette.
"You know I'm like a cat. I can see as well by
night as by day."

Poor Pinocchio! He pretended to be full of
hope; but on the contrary he was beginning to
give up. His strength was ebbing away, and his
breathing grew more difficult. In fact he was almost exhausted, and the shore was still far away.

But he swam on until he was entirely winded;
then he turned to Gepetto and said in a faint
voice:

"Help me, father, or I shall drown!"

Both father and son began to sink, when suddenly they heard a hoarse voice saying:

"Who is going to drown?"

"My poor father and I," gasped the mario-nette.

"I recognize that voice. You are Pinocchio!"

"Yes. And you?"

"I am the Tunny who was your fellow prisoner in the Dog-Fish."

"How did you escape?"

"I followed your lead. You showed me the way, and after you escaped I did also."

"You are just in time, Tunny! I pray you, for the love you bear your Tunny children, to help us, or we are lost!"

"Gladly! Just hang on to my tail, both of you, and let me pull you along. In four minutes I will tow you ashore."

As you can well guess, Gepetto and Pinocchio lost no time in accepting this offer. But instead of holding on to the tail they thought it would be safer to sit down on the back of the Tunny.

"Are we too heavy?" asked Pinocchio.

"Heavy? Not at all! You feel like a couple of sea-shells on my back," replied the polite Tunny, who was large and strong, being about the size of a two-year-old calf.

When they reached the shore, Pinocchio
jumped down and helped his father to land.
Then he turned to the Tunny and said in a voice
which trembled with emotion:

"My friend, you have saved my father. Words
cannot express my gratitude to you. Allow me
to give you a kiss, as a sign of eternal friendship."

The Tunny thrust his nose out of the water,
and Pinocchio kneeling down gave him a very
affectionate kiss. At this token of tender regard,
the poor Tunny, who was not used to such things,
felt so moved that he began to cry like a baby,
and quickly swam away to hide his tears.

Meanwhile day had come. Pinocchio offered
his arm to Gepetto who had barely enough
strength left to stand up, and said to him:

"Lean upon me, father. We will walk ahead
very slowly, and when we are tired we can rest
by the way."

"But where can we go?" asked Gepetto.

"In search of some house where, for charity's
sake, they will give us a crust of bread to eat and
a bunch of straw to lie upon."

They had not gone a hundred paces when they
saw by the roadside two ugly looking fellows ask-

ing alms.   They were the Fox and the Cat, but they had changed so you would hardly have known them.   The Cat, who once pretended to be blind, had now really become so.   The Fox had grown old and was lame, and had lost his tail. The miserable thief had sunk into such depths of poverty that he was at last forced to sell his tail to a peddler, to be used for a brush.

"Oh, Pinocchio!" cried the Fox in a whining voice.   "Give a little aid to two poor wretches!"

"Two poor wretches!" repeated the Cat.

"Good-bye, cheats," said the marionette. "You tricked me once, but you can't catch me again."

"Believe me, Pinocchio.   To-day we are truly poor and miserable!"

"Truly!" repeated the Cat.

"If you are poor, you deserve it.   Good-day to you!"

"Have pity on us, this time!"

"This time!" repeated the Cat.

"Good-bye, cheats.   May you learn wisdom from your suffering!"

So saying, Pinocchio and Gepetto went calmly on their way.   Finally, they came to a roadway which led into the middle of a field, where stood a little house made of thatched straw and with a tiled roof.

"That house must be occupied by some one," said Pinocchio. "Let us go and knock."

They did so.

"Who's there?" called a voice from within.

"We are a poor man and his son who have no shelter or food," replied the marionette.

"Turn the key and the door will open."

Pinocchio obeyed and they entered the house. But they looked all around and saw no one.

"Where is the master of the house?" the boy asked in surprise.

"Here I am."

The two turned quickly and saw on a rafter over their heads no less person than the Talking Cricket.

"Oh, my dear Cricket!" cried Pinocchio in greeting.

"Now I am your 'dear Cricket,' eh? But do you remember the day when you hit me with a hammer?"

"You are right, Cricket! Now it's your turn. Drive me away with a blow of the hammer; but have mercy on my poor father."

"I will have mercy on you both. But I thought it wise to remind you of your own unkindness, in order to show you that, in this world, one must be courteous to all, if one would expect courtesy in the hour of need."

"Right again, Cricket, and I shan't forget it. But tell me, how did you obtain such a nice little house?"

"It was given to me yesterday by a handsome Goat, whose wool was of a beautiful blue color."

"And where did the Goat go?" asked Pinocchio with lively curiosity.

"I do not know."

"When will it return?"

"Never. Yesterday it went away bleating, as if to say, 'Poor Pinocchio! I shall never see him again! The Dog-Fish has devoured him!' "

"Did it really say that? Then it was she! It was my dear Fairy!" said Pinocchio, beginning to cry.

After a while he dried his eyes and made a good bed of straw for the aged Gepetto. Then he asked the Talking Cricket:

"Can you tell me where I can get a glass of milk for my father?"

"Three fields from here you will find a farmer

who owns some cows. Go to him and you'll get your milk."

Pinocchio ran to the farmer and said to him: "May I have a glass of milk for my father?"

"A glass of milk costs one cent," replied the man. "Where's your money?"

"I haven't any."

"Then I haven't any milk. But wait a minute. Maybe we can manage it. Can you work a well-sweep?"

"What is that?"

"It's a thing we use to draw up water out of a well. If you will draw a hundred buckets full, I will give you a glass of milk."

"All right."

The farmer set Pinocchio at work with the well-sweep, and he toiled hard. But before he had drawn his hundred buckets full, he was wet with perspiration from head to foot. He had never felt so tired in all his life.

"This work has always been done for me by a little donkey," said the man; "but to-day the poor beast is sick."

"Will you let me see him?" asked Pinocchio.

"Certainly."

Pinocchio went with him to the stable, and

there stretched out on the straw he saw the donkey dying of hunger and overwork. After looking him in the face, he said to himself, "I think I know that donkey!"   And stooping down he asked in donkey language, "Who are you?"

At this question, the donkey opened his dimming eyes, and answered in a broken voice, "I am Lampwick!" Then he closed his eyes again.

"Oh, poor Lampwick!" said Pinocchio in a low voice. And he took a wisp of hay and offered it to him. But the donkey paid no more attention.

"You seem very sorry about a beast that never cost you anything," said the farmer. "Then how should I feel who am out good money on his account?"

"He was a friend of mine."

"A friend of yours?"

"Yes—a schoolmate."

"That's rich!" shouted the man laughing. "What sort of a schoolmate would a donkey make?"

The marionette felt so ashamed at this, that he made no reply. He took his glass of milk and went back to his father.

37 A Real Boy at Last

From that day on, for five months, Pinocchio rose early every morning to go and work the well-sweep for the farmer. In this way he earned the daily glass of milk which helped to restore the health of his sick father. Not content with that, he learned to weave wicker baskets and hampers, and sold them for enough money to provide for their daily needs. Among other things he bought a nice little wagon in which he took his father out to enjoy the air on fine days.

During the evenings he practiced reading and writing. In a neighboring town he bought a second-hand book for a few cents, and this was used for reading. As for writing he made his own pen out of a piece of scrap-iron, and his own ink from berry juice.

In a word, he behaved so well that he not only made enough money for them both, but also laid aside a small sum to buy new clothes for himself.

One morning he said to his father, "I am going to town to buy myself a new coat and hat and a pair of shoes. When I come back I shall look so fine that you won't know me."

And he laughed and started out in high spirits. He had not gone far, however, when he heard his name called, and turning saw a beautiful Snail climbing over a hedge.

"Don't you know me?" asked the Snail.

"Why it seems to me——" said the marionette, in doubt.

"Don't you remember the Snail who tended

the door for the Fairy with the Blue Hair? I was so slow in coming that you rammed your foot through the panel."

"Oh, yes, I remember now! Tell me quickly, beautiful Snail, where is my good Fairy? What is she doing? Has she forgiven me? Could I go to see her?"

To all these questions the Snail replied with her usual slowness, "I'm sorry to say that the Fairy is ill and in a hospital."

"In a hospital?"

"Alas, yes. A prey to a thousand griefs she fell sick, and is now so poor that she cannot buy a piece of bread."

"Oh, my poor Fairy! my poor Fairy!" wailed Pinocchio. "I wish I had a million dollars to give to her. But all I have in the world you see here in my hand. Take it, good Snail, and hurry to her with it."

"But don't you need it?"

"I was only going to buy some clothes, but what difference does that make? I would sell the very rags off my back to help her. So hasten, good Snail. Come back in a couple of days, and I will try to have something more for her."

The Snail, contrary to her usual way, began to run as swiftly as a lizard.

When Pinocchio went back to the house his father asked, "Where are your clothes?"

"I decided not to buy them to-day. But never mind; there will be plenty of chances."

That night Pinocchio sat up two hours later than usual, and instead of weaving eight baskets he wove sixteen. Very weary, he went to bed and fell asleep. As he slept he dreamed that he saw the Fairy, radiant and smiling, and she bent over and kissed him and said:

"My good Pinocchio! Because of your kind heart I forgive you for all your misdeeds. Boys who help other people so willingly and lovingly deserve praise, even if they are not models in other ways. Always listen to good counsel, and you will be happy."

Here the dream ended, and Pinocchio awoke with his eyes wide open.

Imagine his surprise, now, to discover that he was no longer a wooden marionette! Instead, he had become a real flesh-and-blood boy, just like other boys. He rubbed his eyes and looked around. The bare room in the straw cottage had vanished, and instead he saw a fine sleeping apartment, handsomely furnished. Jumping out of bed, he found laid out for him a beautiful new suit of clothes, with hat and leather boots to match, all of which fitted him perfectly.

When he had dressed himself, with many exclamations of delight, he happened to put his hand into his pocket, and there he found a small ivory purse on which were written these words:

"The Fairy with the Blue Hair returns to her dear Pinocchio the money he sent her, and thanks him for his good heart."

Opening the purse, he found the same number of pieces which he had given away, but instead of copper they were shining gold.

Then he chanced to see himself in a handsome mirror at the other end of the room, and it seemed to him as if it were somebody else. Instead of the silly face, long nose, and rickety joints of a wooden marionette, he beheld a bright, intelligent boy, with brown hair, blue eyes, and fresh, glowing complexion. Indeed, he was as handsome a boy as you would wish to see.

These surprises had happened so close together that Pinocchio did not know whether they were real, or whether he was not still dreaming.

"Where is my dear father?" he cried suddenly.

He ran into the next room, and there found Gepetto hale and hearty, as though he were a young man again. His father felt so well, in fact, that he had set to work again at his trade of wood-carving.

"What has happened, father? How have all these splendid things come about?" cried the boy throwing his arms about his neck.

"It is your reward," replied Gepetto.

"My reward? Why?"

"For your change of conduct. When boys quit being bad and try to be good, they make the whole household happy."

"And the old wooden Pinocchio—where has he gone?"

"There he is," answered Gepetto, pointing to a limp, lifeless wooden doll leaning against a chair with its head hung upon one side, and its legs crossed so that it looked ready to topple over at any moment.

Pinocchio looked at it for a moment; then he said to himself with great satisfaction:

"How funny I was, when I was a marionette! And how glad I am to be a real boy at last!"

Pinocchio

illustrated by Richard Floethe, is a new printing of the

Rainbow Classic edition

Edited under the supervision of May Lamberton Becker

Typesetting by Westcott and Thomson

Interior design by Ernst Reichl

Printed and bound by Arcata

Cover design by Mike Suh